The Star Riders: The Twelve
Victoria Perkins
Copyright 2015 Victoria Perkins
Create Space Edition

Check out these other titles by Victoria Perkins:

Reeves' Island

The Last Summer

Three, Two, One

My Immortal, 'm Cara

This Weak & Idle Theme

The Dragon Three

Check out her official website at

www.vpbooks.com

For my grandparents and parents:
who always encouraged and supported me,
who gave me a love for stories in all forms,
and whose marriages were amazing examples
of Godly love and hard work.

THE STAR RIDERS:

THE TWELVE

Prologue

The world ended in a blaze of holy light, cleansing the universe in preparation for what was to come next. Yet, even as the celebrations began, a soft command was given, and with a rustle of feathers, the appointed one took flight. The war may have ended here, but that only meant the danger for the other worlds grew. His job was clear. The twelfth must be found, the circle completed. Eleven had been left behind to stand between the darkness and humanity. If they fell, evil would consume every other world and billions of souls would be lost forever.

He closed his eyes and felt for the crack between universes. He was one of only a handful of his kind who could do this, who could travel like one of *them*.

There. He could feel it.

He stretched his arms over his head, speeding up. He tucked his wings tight against his body and began to spin. As he cut through the fabric of space, he could feel the darkness behind him. Following. Time was growing short.

He put on a burst of speed. This was not the time to worry about conserving energy. He had to reach them before they tried to go home. He had to make them see.

This was his greatest mission, the one he had been created to carry out. He could not fail.

Chapter One

Tempest

I held the flashlight between my teeth as I inserted the thin metal file into the lock. Slow inhales through my nose, slow exhales around the cheap plastic. My hands were steady, fingers never faltering as they maneuvered the workings of the lock. My pulse remained slow and regular. For all my body knew, I was relaxing with a good book, not attempting to break into my court-appointed therapist's office to read my file.

I needed to know what Dr. Rosabelle was going to recommend tomorrow so I could prepare. And by prepare, I meant figure out which way I was going to run.

I heard the security guard coming down the hallway and pushed back the sliver of panic wanting to break through. The lock clicked, and I slipped inside just as Harold, the night guard, rounded the corner. If I did my job right, no one would know I'd been here, and Harold would still have a job come morning. He was a nice enough guy; I didn't want him to get fired because of me.

I turned off the flashlight and waited for Harold to disappear down the hallway. Once I was sure he was far enough away, I turned my light back on and headed for the good doctor's computer. Her password was disturbingly easy to crack – a psychiatrist using Skinner as a password deserved to have her computer hacked. Freud and Jung got me into the patients' general folder and my personal file respectively.

Tempest Anne Black.

I skipped over the session notes. I knew what I'd told her and anything particularly important would be included in my assessment. I opened the file and began to read.

Seventeen. Mother Susanna Black, deceased. Father, unknown.

I skimmed over the medical reports of the abuse and injuries I'd sustained in my various foster homes as well as the list of arrests starting at age eight.

Been there, done that.

I didn't need a report to remind me I'd been in juvie seven times in nine years. Petty stuff. Mostly running from whatever home the state put me in, but there'd also been some B&E and one incident of hacking before I'd gotten too good to be caught.

My latest stint had been three months and I'd been out for six weeks, but was on probation, hence the weekly meetings with Dr. Rosabelle. Tomorrow, she was supposed to tell a judge if she thought they should skip the foster home, and send me straight back to juvie until I turned eighteen. No way was I going back for another seven months. Not when I kept getting thrown into solitary for defending myself.

I kept reading.

Assessment.

That's what I wanted.

Miss Black is highly intelligent, but without a measured IQ as she refuses all attempts to test her. Her poor grades are most likely the result of boredom rather than lack of understanding. Her disdain for authority figures and belief that she is the smartest person in the room also contributes to her schooling issues. Prior testing has diagnosed Miss Black as having Attention Deficit Hyperactive Disorder with Obsessive Compulsive and Narcissistic tendencies. I concur with these findings. I also believe her to be suffering from some sort of social anxiety disorder or perhaps even a form of autism. The former are all treatable with the proper medications. Therein lies the problem, as Miss Black refuses to take her medication...

I closed the file. I didn't need to read any more. I already knew what it was going to say. I needed supervision to ensure I took my meds. Meds I didn't want and was pretty sure I didn't need. Since I couldn't be trusted to take the prescribed medication, or not to run from any home I was put in, I'd be back in juvie until I turned eighteen in April.

I only half paid attention to what I was doing as I tucked

my file under my arm. It'd end up in a fire at some point tonight. The other half of my brain was going over my plan. I'd always been a good multi-tasker.

I wasn't really surprised by the good doctor's findings. I knew how people saw me. Wild dark brown curls that looked like they needed tamed as much as the rest of me. Jade-colored eyes that I'd been told were arrogant and cold, which was fine with me because that wasn't a bad image to portray in my life. I was only average height, but I was strong.

Once I was safely outside, I pulled off the knit cap I'd used to prevent leaving behind any hair, and my curls tumbled out. They brushed against my bare skin, falling to bit past my shoulder-blades.

A cool breeze blew, making me wish for a moment I'd brought a coat to wear over my tank top. Autumn had come to Ohio and, with it, much cooler weather. Not for the first time, I wished my mom would've died someplace warm. At least then I would've been stuck with sunshine instead of the unpredictability of Northeastern Ohio weather. Not that I hadn't tried going someplace warmer. I'd just kept getting caught. This time, however, I was going to do what I hadn't had the courage to do before.

I was going to erase myself.

I wasn't a coward, but taking myself off the grid was

extreme. When I was done, Tempest Black would cease to exist, and she was the only thing I had left of my mother, of my past. I didn't even know what my mom had looked like because the only picture of her had been taken at the morgue for their records, and I'd only seen it once. That wasn't the image I wanted in my head when I thought of her.

My lips flattened and I knew if I could see them, they'd be white. I couldn't really say I loved my mother because I'd never met her, but I'd spent enough time as a little kid fantasizing about who she'd been to love the idea of her. I never wanted to think about any of that anymore. Mourning over what might have been was stupid, and it hurt too much.

And I avoided pain at all costs.

I glanced at the Coptic cross tattoo on the inside of my right wrist. Emotional pain anyway. The physical kind actually made me feel alive. Not so much so that I'd gotten into self-harm, but I didn't exactly react to pain the way most people did. My other tattoo was partially visible under the scoop neck of my black tank. I'd gotten my favorite quote inked across my collarbone the last time I'd run. "To thine own self be true" had always resonated with me. I had plans for a couple more once I had the money.

I jogged up the stairs of the condemned apartment building where I'd been hiding since my session with Dr. Rosabelle had ended yesterday.

I pushed the other thoughts aside. I didn't have the time to be introspective. I had work to do.

No one else lived on the third floor. It wasn't exactly safe. The whole building wasn't in the best of shape, but there were parts of the ceiling on the third floor that were completely gone. I didn't really mind. It was still better than some of the other places I'd lived.

I didn't have much to pack. Another perk of being me. The one change of clothes I'd managed to smuggle out of the group home where I'd been staying, and a box that had belonged to my mom, but I could never figure out how to open. The box wasn't here though. I'd put it in a plastic bag and buried it behind the building. I couldn't take it with me now, but I promised myself I'd be back for it someday.

I left the flat pillow and threadbare blanket for the next runaway who needed a place to crash. I didn't want to take up extra room in my bag since I didn't know how far I was going, and it wasn't too cold yet. I felt a vague tug inside me, a pull I'd been ignoring for the past three weeks. I couldn't explain it, and I didn't know why it was happening. All I knew was something wanted me to go West.

When I left, I didn't look back or even bother to go by any of the dozen places I'd lived in Wycliffe. There wasn't any reason to. None of those places were home. No place was. And once I spent some time in a local internet café, I'd check out that western tug and see if I could find myself a place to disappear.

Not a home. People like me had stops, places to crash, but never homes.

Chapter Two

Bram

I hurled my knife at the final demon as it charged towards me, and the blade lodged directly between its eyes with a satisfying thud. Its momentum carried it forward until it skidded to a stop a few inches from my feet. It was an ugly brute, one of those that preferred to show its true nature rather than shielding itself in the illusion of light. I would rather have fought a thousand of those than the other kind, the ones who pretended to be something they weren't. Not because I actually saw the illusion. My kind could see through it.

I nudged the creature with my toe, my wings spread, ready to react if it should so much as twitch. It didn't though. As much power as I'd laced my weapon with, no demon could have survived. I pulled my wings in as I crouched next to it and yanked the blade out of its face. I made a face at the stench. It didn't matter how many of these creatures I'd killed, I never got used to the stink.

I knew it as an *excoriator* demon, a kind I'd seen hundreds, if not thousands, of times before. Still, I studied it for a moment, wondering what kind of angel it had been before it had been corrupted. Perhaps one of music or even one of the guard. It was nearly impossible to tell. Even the ones who pretended they'd maintained their prior glory could be lying about their former rank and position. Lucifer was not nicknamed The Father of Lies on hundreds of worlds because of his honesty.

"Was that the last?"

I looked up, trying to remember the name of the young man with the slight French accent. This had been the first assignment where the eleven of us had been sent together. Usually, we went in pairs or groups of four to six. I'd never heard of a group this large being sent to clear out a single nest of demons.

"It was," I said as I stood.

The speaker was at least four inches short than me, putting him at a little under six feet tall, but his shoulders were broader than mine, his arms and chest more muscular.

I tried to remember his name. Sandy brown hair, bright green eyes...well, eye actually. He had a patch over the place where his left eye had been. Now I remembered.

Grady Verne-Frost, descended from founders Jules Verne's and Robert Frost's families. A cousin of mine somewhere in the Frost family line. Rumor among the Qaniss was that Grady had lost his eye fighting a demon on our home world when he'd been fifteen. I hadn't asked. He was eighteen now, and bonded to one of the twins. I couldn't remember which one.

"Losses?" I asked.

"None on our side," he said. He looked down at the demon at my feet. "Should we burn them where they fell or make a bonfire?"

I looked around and found the rest of the group watching me. I was the eldest of us, older than Lucan by a week, but I knew it wasn't my age that made them look to me, or that I had been battling demons since I was twelve. After seven years, I was used to the way people watched me, looked to me for answers.

"Human population?" I asked.

"Not for thirty miles or so," the youngest of our group answered, her thick Scottish brogue making her sound even younger than she was. Three years younger than me, with short ginger girls and a clear eagerness to prove herself, she was going to be one to watch. That enthusiasm could easily become a liability in the field.

"Tady Wells," she reminded me.

Another distant cousin then. A halfer if I remembered correctly. Her mother was Scottish, a non-Qaniss who'd met her father in the Highlands. For a moment, I wondered if this was her first mission and who'd be going over the details of her experience with her when we returned home.

No matter. I pushed the thought aside Tady wasn't mine to

train, nor bonded with me. Judging by the way the athletic young man next to her kept his dark green eyes on her, she was his.

"Burn the bodies where they lie," I said. "No need to waste time if we can leave their ashes be."

Out of the corner of my eye, I saw a petite blonde making gestures to her bonded, a handsome young man with bronzed skin and clear blue eyes. Them I knew by reputation, and all of it good.

Emilia Bronte-Anderson and Harrison Lovecraft. She'd been raised in London, England; him in Anchorage, Alaska. They'd been only five when they had claimed each other, the youngest of our kind to ever be bonded. An accident when they were ten had left Harrison all but deaf, retaining only very minor hearing in one ear. Emilia had rescued him, or so the story went.

We set about our business. With eleven of us, setting fire to the thirty or so demons we'd dispatched didn't take very long, but we were required by law to ensure the bodies were reduced to dust. We couldn't risk humans discovering any of the remains. Some of our ancestors hadn't been so careful, and there were worlds where demon remains had been, and were still being, used to 'prove' various theories and mythologies.

"Hi!"

I looked down to see Tady grinning up at me. She had a smudge of soot across her nose and her wings were twitching. Like all of us, hers had the same coloring as her hair and eyes. In her case, they were a deep, rustic red, streaked with the same browns, greens and golds that made up her eyes. I nodded at her, hoping she'd take the hint that I didn't really want to talk. I wasn't trying to be rude or anything, but I worked alone. I was the only one of our kind who did, and I liked it.

"Our mothers would be third cousins twice removed," she said. "Grady's yer cousin too, right?"

"So is Fynn." I gestured towards the seventeen year-old standing at the edge of the group. He had dark blond hair, baby blue eyes, and the kind of face that was going to make him look like a kid for the rest of his life. Despite our relation, we looked nothing alike except in our lean builds. He'd been raised in Australia and had the accent to prove it. My hair was black, my eyes slate gray. I didn't have a youthful, pretty-boy face, though I'd been told I was good-looking.

Not that I had time for any of that nonsense. I wasn't interested in romance or love. I was good at my job and intended to stick with it until it eventually killed me. Which, for my kind, was generally sooner rather than later.

"I've been doin' some genealogy research."

Great. She was one of those, obsessed with the lineage. The only thing that made who we came from important was it indicated how powerful a particular Qaniss was. The older the founder ancestor, the stronger the bloodline.

Then again, her research made sense considering how some Qaniss looked down on those who only had one Qaniss parent. A halfer like her. I'd never understood that kind of thinking since pretty much every bloodline had outsiders marry in. It was the only way we'd survived.

"Yer descended from three founders." She kept going as I stared at the fire. "Including the original, Wilhelm Grimm."

"He wasn't the original," I corrected her, amused despite myself at how the German name sounded in a Scottish accent.

"Aye, I know," she said. "But since we dinna have any descendants from the original, Wilhelm's line is considered the oldest."

My mouth twisted into a scowl, humor forgotten. I knew where she was going with this and I didn't like it.

"So that means yer next in line to lead us."

"My father will choose a successor when the time comes for him to step down." I kicked some dirt at a smoldering corpse. "If you'll excuse me, I need to do something before we leave." I didn't wait for a response, but headed off towards the trees.

I rubbed the mark on the inside of my right wrist. It was the source of my power, the way it had been infused into me when I was twelve. I sometimes wondered if the others felt it burning and aching after a fight, or if that was something eased by the bonding.

I ducked behind some trees and leaned against one, closing my eyes as my thumb massaged the throbbing spot. I could feel a headache starting to form. I couldn't let any of the others see it. If anyone of the Qaniss elders discovered I was suffering any sort of pain, they might try to strip me of my powers. I couldn't let that happen. I knew they were always keeping a close watch on me. One of those ten might even be reporting back.

Everything had changed the moment I'd gone from the poor kid who hadn't found a bonded, to Bram Grimm, the only Qaniss to survive the tattoo without a bond. The only one who'd ever demanded to even try it, actually. My father had only done it because I'd threatened to attempt it myself, a crime punishable by death. He had preferred that if I was going to die, I'd do it trying to uphold our family line. He'd never expected me to survive. Seven years later, and I still didn't know if I'd expected it either. No one knew how I did it either. The power was meant to be shared.

"Bram!"

My eyes flew open.

I didn't recognize the voice, but that didn't matter. I knew the tone.

Something was wrong.

I ran back towards the clearing, unsheathing my longest knife as I went. Adrenaline coursed through my veins, preparing me for anything.

More demons.

Human authorities – though we wouldn't need weapons for those. Diplomacy usually worked. Well, usually good enough until we could escape.

I was ready to deal with whatever assault the enemy threw my way.

I skidded to a halt between Tady and her bonded.

The one thing I hadn't expected was *him*.

Chapter Three

Tempest

I laid on my back, my pack serving as a pillow, and I stared up at the stars.

When I'd been seven, my class had taken a trip to the planetarium. From the moment I'd seen those stars, swirling overhead, I'd been hooked. There'd been something peaceful about them, the specks of light in velvet black, promises of other worlds and other lives. I didn't believe in little green men, but the idea of possibilities made me hope for something more, even if only in my dreams.

I snorted a laugh. I must've been more tired than I'd realized if I was bringing those memories up again. I still loved the stars, but now I appreciated them from a purely aesthetic perspective. They were truly beautiful, but there wasn't anything special up there.

I yawned and pulled my jacket more tightly around me. Western Ohio wasn't any warmer than Northeastern, but at least I was going in the right direction. The tug inside me was still there, and I'd already decided I'd go until it stopped. Maybe I'd end up in Hawaii.

A plane ticket, however, would require ID, and I hadn't gotten any yet.

I was still getting used to the fact that I didn't exist. I held up my hand, looking at my fingers in the dim night light. Yesterday, my prints would've pulled up all kinds of stuff. Today, there'd be nothing. Any computer connected to the internet or networked to a computer that was online, they were all wiped. My case worker, parole officer, doctors, people in the system with me, all of them could say they knew me, remembered me, but there'd be no record of Tempest Black.

I felt a faint pang, and pushed it away. I hadn't felt that in a while, the wild and completely pointless thought that I needed to be able to be found online so my dad could find me. So any family could find me.

I reminded myself that, after seventeen years, if no one had shown up, no one would. I was on my own. Like always.

And it was okay. It was more than okay. I was good at being on my own.

I was still telling myself that when I fell asleep, huddled under a coat I'd snagged from a thrift store drop-off about ten miles ago.

****

A sharp pain in my side pulled me out of a fairly light sleep. Instinctively, I rolled the opposite direction, pulling my feet underneath me as I went. I automatically ended up in a crouch, ready to fight. I was glad I'd been using the jacket as a blanket and hadn't been wearing it. Movement was much easier in my tank top.

The man who'd kicked me laughed, and it wasn't difficult to see why. He was huge, easily six foot three or four, and probably twice as wide. Judging by the scars on the guy's face, he was no stranger to violence.

Fortunately, neither was I.

I had my own scars to prove it.

I put my hand at the small of my back without taking my eyes off of the man. The switchblade I kept there didn't look like much, but I was good with it.

"Move on." I put as much steel into the words as I could.

"How about I don't." The man took a slow look around the spot I'd chosen to sleep. "I like it here."

I cursed myself for picking the overgrown backyard of an abandoned house. It had seemed like a good idea last night. The house was little more than a burnt-out shell, but it had hidden me from the road. Now, that was a problem. I could hear a couple cars passing by, probably commuters heading into the town, but none of them could see me.

Most people would've pulled out the knife and made a threat, but I didn't. I'd learned at a young age that the last thing for me to do when being confronted was to show I had a weapon. If someone was trying to kill me, they didn't deserve a warning.

"Are you gonna make this hard on yourself?" The man took a step towards me and I wrapped my fingers around the handle of the switchblade.

I'd had it since the Shaw house, and I'd used it before. I didn't want to use it again, but I had a bad feeling this guy wasn't going to give me much of a choice.

I bared my teeth at him and shifted my weight so I'd be able to move quickly when he came at me. "What do you think?"

"I was hoping you'd say that."

He was faster than I'd anticipated and as I threw myself to the side, I knew I hadn't moved fast enough. His hand closed around my ankle and I fell forward. I managed to break my fall, but it meant I lost my grip on my knife, and pain jolted up my arms. I twisted, trying to get free, but he laughed and grabbed at my other foot. I heard him swear as my foot made contact with some part of his body, but I didn't try to look to see where. I needed to find my knife.

Then, suddenly, his grip was gone. Before I could react, the air was driven from my lungs as weight dropped onto my back. Sharp pain went through my scalp and radiated down my neck as he yanked my head back.

His breath was hot and foul as he spoke against my ear. Seriously, it was like he'd eaten a skunk. I gagged.

"I'm gonna have fun with you."

My hands scrabbled against the ground, searching for anything I could use. The man was running his mouth, telling me all the things he was going to do to me. I ignored him. I'd heard worse.

His fingers wrapped around my throat and began to squeeze. I forgot about my knife as panic flooded me. I struggled, scratching and clawing at his arm and hand, but couldn't get skin. I gasped, trying to get air as his hand tightened. Images flashed through my head, driving my fear.

Spots dancing behind my eyes.

The pressure of a body against mine.

Pain.

Blood.

Something hard and familiar brushed my fingers, cutting through the panic enough for me to realize what it was. My lungs were burning and I knew I only had a seconds before I passed out. I fumbled with the switch. I felt it give and gathered the last of my remaining strength.

I drove the blade into his forearm, barely registering the tip of the knife go into my shoulder as it came out through his arm. The fingers around my neck loosened and I gasped, my vision clearing. I yanked out the knife and slashed behind me again.

Suddenly, the weight on me vanished and the man let out a stream of impressive expletives. I rolled, kicking my legs as I went.

A hand in my hair yanked me to my feet and I cried out, partially in pain, but also because I was pissed. I let myself be angry. Let it give me strength.

A blow to my ribs sent fresh pain through me, but I managed to keep hold of my knife this time. He hit me again and I buried the blade in his side. He cursed and dropped me.

Somehow, I managed to keep my feet under me and stabbed him again. I took a step backwards, blood dripping from my knife.

"Move on." I repeated my previous comment.

My voice was rough, the words painful. I didn't let it show though. He had to think I could keep going until I killed him.

He glared at me, then looked down at the blood seeping between his fingers. "Not worth it," he muttered, adding a foul name at the end.

I waited until he'd walked away before grabbing my bag and making my way around the house. I cut a wide berth around it, not stupid enough to get close and be caught if the guy was waiting. He wasn't there, but I still didn't pause to wipe the blade and pocket my knife. I did it while I walked. Checking my injuries would have to wait.

I wasn't sure how far I'd walked when I saw a sign that made me smile. Defiance. Great name for a town. I kinda wanted to stay so I could say I lived in Defiance – not that I had anyone to tell – but I knew it was only a momentary bit of wishful thinking. I needed to keep going. Aside from the pull to the west, I knew someone like me would stick out like a sore thumb. That was why most runaways who didn't have family or friends to go to ended up in the big cities where they could disappear, blend in better. None of them had ever appealed to me. Probably because I didn't like people very much. I didn't think I had to worry about it though. For some reason I couldn't explain, I doubted this tug inside me was going to take me to a city.

I stopped at a gas station and avoided the attendant as I made my way around to where the bathrooms were located. A little place like this, people were bound to notice a stranger, especially one with ink and injuries like me.

As soon as I looked in the mirror, I was glad I'd avoided people. I was dirty and looked like, well, like I'd been in a fight. The side of my face was swollen from where it had been slammed into the ground, and I had scrapes I hadn't felt until now when I saw them.

I peeled off the jacket, wincing as it pulled on the wound. I muttered a curse as I looked at the drying blood coating my skin and stiffening my shirt. The cut was less than an inch wide, but I suspected it was deeper than I'd originally thought. I could feel the burn and ache deep in the muscle. I really hoped that guy hadn't had any diseases. If he had, I was in trouble. Downside of being non-existent: medical treatment wasn't really going to be an option.

I stripped off my shirt and let it soak in the sink while I cleaned up. The cut was still bleeding, but I knew I wasn't going to have to worry about people staring at the make-shift bandage I was about to make, because they'd be looking at the clear hand-shaped bruise on my neck.

Well, they'd be looking at that, my bruised face, or the jagged scar running from my right temple down to the dimple in my cheek. I hardly saw it anymore. It had been a part of me for years.

As I cleaned up the wound, my eyes flicked to my reflection. I had other scars, burn and whip marks on my back, that were mostly covered by my shirt. They were newer than the one on my face, but I didn't try to hide them either. I wasn't ashamed of my scars. They were evidence that I'd survived.

I pressed some paper towels to my shoulder and adjusted the strap on my bra so it held the towels in place. Then I took a look at my jacket. It was black leather, so at least it wouldn't stain. I turned it inside out and began working on cleaning the inside while I let my top drain excess water.

When the jacket was as clean as I was going to get it, I set it aside and wrung out my tank top. It was still wet, though not dripping, when I pulled it on. I made a face as the cloth clung to my skin. I had a dry shirt in my bag, but it'd be easier for it to dry on me than it would be in the bag, and it would keep the rest of my clothes from getting wet.

I left my hair down as I gathered my bag and jacket. It was going to be chilly if the sun stayed hidden and my hair would help keep me warm enough while I walked. And it'd obscure my face. No need to give anyone anything to remember.

"Hey!" A man called after me as I hurried through the store.

I ignored him. If he followed, I'd pretend I was deaf. It wouldn't be the first time. When I was eleven, I'd made a friend with another orphan, a deaf girl named Eliana. The two of us had decided it'd be fun to 'switch' and pretend I was deaf and she could hear. We'd gotten away with it for six months before someone had figured it out. Fortunately, I didn't have to employ that particular ploy this time. I kept walking and no one followed.

Now, I just needed to find a ride heading West. Until then,

I'd walk.

****

It took me nearly a week to reach Colorado, and then a day or so to fine-tune my sense of direction to find where the pull wanted me to go. Nearly two weeks after I left Ohio, I found myself in Fort Prince, Colorado, a college town near the base of the Rocky Mountains. I still didn't know why I was here, or even how long I was supposed to stay, but as I stood by the sign that welcomed me, I knew whatever was calling for me was here.

I looked down at myself as I headed into town. I was filthy and the journey had done a number on my clothes. A college town seemed like a great place to hide, but first I needed to clean up. I could pass for a college student, but at the moment, I looked exactly like what I was. A homeless kid.

I'd arrived in the middle of the fall semester, which made it a bit more difficult to take what I needed, but I'd manage. Back in Ohio, I'd often stopped by Wycliffe University when students had been moving in or out. With all the chaos, it had been easy to snatch something here or there. Today, I was looking for either a laundromat, or a way into one of the dorms. Someone, somewhere, had to be doing laundry.

I waited for someone to open the door, then slipped inside

after them. I kept my head down and eyes open. This college dorm layout didn't seem too much different than Wycliffe U, so when I found the door to the basement, I took it. I hadn't gone more than a couple feet when I smelled detergent and fabric softener.

I peeked inside. I could see three dryers going, one with only five minutes left. Perfect. I took a step into the room and confirmed it was empty. I didn't know how much time I had, so I worked fast, finding some of what I needed in the dryer, and stealing a bag to carry what I'd taken.

For the next half hour, I picked my way through the laundry rooms of several different doors, giving myself time to scope out the rest of the layout of the campus as I went. I never took more than one or two items from each person, and never more than four from the same dorm. Still, by the time I'd finished, I had two full changes of clothes which included two layers of shirts for each, and that was more than enough for me. Then it was time for the more dangerous part of my little trip.

I needed a shower. Badly. I'd managed a sponge bath or two at various rest-stops, but the last actual shower I'd taken had been back in Ohio right before I'd broken into my therapist's office. I'd known there was a possibility I wouldn't be getting one for a while, and was glad now I'd done it. I could only imagine how bad I'd smell if I hadn't.

I picked one of the two girls' dorms and headed inside. I didn't mind raiding guys clothes and, in a pinch, I'd have used one of their showers, claiming to be someone's drunken fling if I was caught, but I couldn't count on men to not take a naked woman in the shower as an invitation. I supposed a woman could always proposition me, but I hadn't found that to be the case in the past, at least not as aggressively as men.

I was standing under the hot spray, reveling in the feel of days of dirt and grim sloughing away, when I heard someone enter the bathroom. More than one someone. They were carrying on a conversation and I strained to hear if someone had discovered my thefts.

"I'm telling you, Garnet, he said he saw falling stars a couple nights ago."

"Falling stars landing in the mountains?" The second girl sounded skeptical. "I think Manny was messing with you."

"Probably," the first girl agreed. "But a bunch of us are going to head up to his family's cabin this weekend to check it out."

Something in my stomach twisted and I felt the tug again. Falling stars in the mountains. Even if I hadn't felt compelled to go, I would've wanted to anyway. I knew the odds were low of there being anything to find, but it wasn't like I had any other plans or anything. I was following my gut for the simple reason that it gave me something to do rather than aimless wandering. I hated not having a purpose.

I frowned as I washed my hair with stolen shampoo.

Sometimes I thought that was the worst part of being someone like me. The pointlessness of it all.

My grades had never been the best, and with my juvie record, no college was going to accept me. Not that I had any idea what I wanted to do or if I needed college to do it. I was smart, but I didn't have any direction.

Most of the time, kids without a clue would've had parents or friends or teachers to encourage them, to try to help them. Kids without parents or friends, kids whose teachers didn't like them or were too tired to care, we didn't have anyone to guide us. We had to figure it all out on our own.

The girls' voices faded as they left, and I idly wondered if they had families who helped them figure out what they wanted to do with their lives. Probably. They sounded way too well-adjusted.

I pushed thoughts of the girls and their families out of my mind. I had other things to think about. I may not have had some big plans about a career or a future, but I did know at least the next step I had to take.

I had to get to the mountains. The ones where the stars had

fallen. I had no clue what any of it meant, only that my gut said I needed to go.

First things first.

To get to the mountains, I'd need transportation. I sighed. So much for relaxing. Once I got dressed, I was going to have to steal a car.

Chapter Four

Bram

It was autumn when we'd arrived, cutting through the spaces between with little difficulty. The world we'd come from and the world we were going to were close together, which made it easier. Not close physically, of course, because that wasn't how it worked. They were close along the same timeline. It was always easier to move when that was the case, especially if we weren't coming from...

I pushed the thought aside. I didn't want to think about other worlds, about *that* world.

I looked around at the others and knew they were thinking the same thing. We'd come here immediately, found an empty cabin...and waited. None of us had talked much, not even Tady. There wasn't really anything to say.

I knew their names now. I made sure I did. Their names. Who they were descended from. Which ones were bonded. I had to know all of it now. I was the last of my line. We all were. It was my job.

I looked at them again, counting them off in my head as if I needed to reassure myself no more of us had been lost.

There were the seventeen year-old Poe twins, Annabella and Leigh. Identical from their golden blonde hair to their coal black eyes. The only way to tell them apart were their tattoos. I'd only seen the top two letters of the one on Annabella's, but considering her lineage, it wasn't hard to figure out the "Nev" was the beginning of the word "Nevermore." Leigh had a raven on her left ankle.

Well, the tattoos and their wings. They were opposites. Annabella's black streaked with golden yellow and Leigh's the opposite.

Annabella was bonded to Grady, Leigh to Lucan Bronte-Carroll. The four of them were rarely apart.

Then there were Emilia and Harrison who were handling things with an almost scary calm.

Next were Tady and her bonded, Bair Austen-Stoker. Neither one of them had even tried to hide how much they'd been crying.

The final pair were Fynn and his bonded, Kassia Coleridge-Dickens, a tough-looking seventeen year-old with chin-length black hair and bright purple streaks. Their eyes were red, but their cheeks dry.

That was it. Those ten and me. We were it. The only ones left.

I stood up suddenly, but no one really paid any attention. They were all too wrapped up in their own grief and the grief of their bonded.

I didn't have anyone to share my burden. I was alone.

The cabin we'd found was high in the Rocky Mountains and this late in the year, the nights were cold enough to merit a fire. The place had been stocked with perishables and a bit of firewood, but we'd run out of the wood. The sun was almost down, and the embers we had going were going to need some more fuel.

Driving a piece of sharp metal repeated into various objects sounded like as good a way to clear my mind as any.

I didn't bother taking a jacket. I could smell the snow coming, still at least a week away, but I'd be working up a sweat shortly. Besides, it had to be subzero before I got cold. All Qaniss ran hotter than normal. Most of us reasoned it was so we didn't have to worry about wearing bulky clothing when we fought. I was about five degrees hotter. I always figured it was because I carried extra power. Whatever the reason, it meant I was in short sleeves when I started splitting wood.

The rhythm was soothing, the physical exertion comforting. I'd spent my entire life doing training and working out. We rarely ever took time off. While the Qaniss had slightly faster reflexes, sharper senses and healed twice as fast as regular humans, we weren't invulnerable or some sort of superhero who was automatically buff. And we definitely weren't immune to permanent injuries or scars. My own body was as much proof of that as the others.

I'd been working for nearly an hour before I paused and pulled off my soaking shirt. Steam was billowing off of me, and the cool air felt good against my skin. I tossed the shirt on the wood I'd already cut. I was already going to need to wash it. Qaniss always traveled with a spare set of clothes, never knowing if we'd need to change out of something bloody before the locals caught on. Now, they were the only clothes I owned.

I stretched my wings out, using them to generate a bit of air around my body before they disappeared into my back. Even with hundreds of years of study, we'd never been able to figure out exactly how it worked. I wiped the back of my hand across my forehead, and let out a bitter laugh.

Two sets of clothes, and the weapons I'd had strapped to me when I'd left. That was it.

I'd seen stories over the years, interviews with people who'd experienced the loss of their homes and neighborhoods, generally due to natural disasters. They always talked about how they only had the clothes on their backs. I had a bit more than that, but I'd lost far more than they had.

I sat down on the stump I'd been using as a cutting block. I could feel the shield I'd put up around all of those feelings start to crack. I'd had to be strong these last couple days, leading us, the remnant. I was my father's child, the last of the Grimms. It was my place to lead. It was also a good excuse not to have to think about the message Viator had brought. The message that had changed everything.

A flash of white light blinded us, followed by the unmistakable crack of someone coming into the world. I shifted into a fighting stance, waiting to see if it would be friend or foe. The others had seen the streaks of light and the ripple in the air that always preceded the entrance to another world, and it had been then they'd called for me. The moment my eyes adjusted, however, I knew I could put away my knife.

He was pleasant-looking, but not so much he would attract attention. His clothes were plain, automatically adapting to the current world's fashion. We didn't have that ability, but then again, we weren't him. And since he wasn't one of us, but had traveled between worlds, I knew immediately who he was even though I'd never met him.

Viator. One of only a few Adonai's angels who had the ability to travel between worlds. And the only one who'd been assigned to the Qaniss.

"Do you have a message for us?" I asked.

One look into those piercing blue eyes and I suddenly wished I had stayed away. Viator brought us nothing good. I could feel it.

"Eleven of Qaniss, descendants of the founders, warriors of Adonai, I bring news of the end."

I heard one of the others make a noise but I didn't look to see which one. My hands curled into fists while I waited for him to finish.

"The time has come," he continued. "Adonai has called his people home."

It was one of the twins who spoke this time, but I didn't know which. "Our world?"

"Gone," he said, his expression impassive, as if he hadn't just told us that everyone and everything we knew were no more. "Your people are home. Their reward has begun."

"Donna nobis pacem."

I thought the voice was Leigh's, but I wasn't sure. It didn't matter though. I didn't think any of us were going to be granted peace any time soon.

A broken sound came from behind me, and I wondered if any of my companions hadn't only lost parents and siblings, but a partner, fiancée, or spouse. I prayed none had lost a child. We were young, but Qaniss married early in life. Very few of my kind lived to be too old to fight.

Or, at least, it used to be that way. None were left now. I knew, in my head, this wasn't a bad thing. They were with Adonai now, enjoying paradise. No more sickness, no more death. They would live forever at His side. My heart, however, didn't agree. I wasn't with them. I was left. Alone.

"Jehovah has sent me to you."

"To take us home as well?" Tady asked, hope evident in her voice.

"To give you a choice."

I had known before he'd said it what our options would be, and when he'd spoken he'd confirmed my suspicions. He could take us home, to paradise. We would be with our families and friends, never again have to fight against demons, never see the people we loved killed or corrupted. Our work would be done. We would have peace.

Or we could fight.

With our world gone, the forces of darkness would focus more of their attention on the other worlds, desperate to claim as many souls as possible before the inevitable end of all things. Some would be able to resist, but without the Qaniss, millions upon millions would be forever lost.

We knew the angels outnumbered the demons by a third, but the end of our world meant the angels would be called home too. We were the only ones who stood between the people of thousands of worlds and total darkness.

But it was more than that, we had learned. There was a reason the eleven of us had been sent away together, a reason why Adonai had commanded it. There was a prophecy...

A branch cracked in the woods behind me, immediately pulling me from my thoughts. I jumped up, my hand automatically going to my waist as the smell hit me. But my sword wasn't there. Nor were my knives. They were back in the cabin. My wings snapped out as I grabbed the ax and turned, ready to kill whatever was there.

Except it was a girl. A dark-haired girl with a jagged scar across her right cheek.

"Duck!" I barked the order even as I raised my arm.

I let the ax fly, and it thudded into the demon that had been sneaking up behind her. I hit it right in the forehead, but I wasn't taking any chances. Not with a *vihane surma*.

I ignored the woman who was staring at me and went straight to the demon. It didn't move as I yanked on the ax handle and then proceeded to chop of the demon's head. I continued to ignore her as she started to curse fluently and colorfully, including a couple words I'd never heard before.

"Hey! I'm talking to–" She grabbed my arm, but as I turned, I heard a thunk and she crumpled to the ground.

I looked down at the now-unconscious young woman on the forest floor. I didn't registered what she looked like or what she was wearing though. All I could see was the Coptic cross tattooed on the inside of her right wrist. A tattoo matching mine exactly.

Chapter Five

Tempest

It was surprisingly easy to steal a car in Fort Prince, and that almost made me feel bad for doing it.

Almost.

Insurance should cover the loss if the cops didn't find the car, and they'd have to be pretty bad at their job if they didn't. I'd left it in the parking lot of a ski lodge a few miles outside of Fort Prince, too far for me to have walked. I assumed the cops would be searching for the thief, but I doubted this would be the first place they'd look, but even if they had, they'd be looking for another missing car or maybe even a person walking down the road. No one in their right mind would walk higher up the mountain in the middle of fall.

It was a good thing I wasn't in my right mind.

I'd stolen some warmer clothes before I'd left, and I was generally a bit warmer than most people, but even the layers couldn't keep me from shivering by the time I was halfway up the mountain. I had absolutely no clue where I was going, and the path I was following didn't look like anything more than an animal trail, but the feeling inside me wouldn't go away. If anything, it grew stronger the further I went.

The light was beginning to fade when I heard a sound. It

was faint, but distinct. It wasn't the cracking of branches, but a thudding sound. In the back of my mind, it nagged at me, like it was a sound I should know. I worried at it while I walked, giving myself something to think of other than the fact that I was starting to lose sensation in my toes. I was closing in on it when I finally put a name to the sound.

Someone was splitting wood.

For a reason I didn't understand, my heart gave a hard thump, and I began to walk faster. I was focused on the sound, more focused than I'd ever been on any one thing. I was dimly aware of the light fading fast, of the sounds of animals scurrying around for the night. Part of me felt like there was something behind me, something I should know, but I couldn't stop to suss it out. I had to get to wherever this pull inside me was taking me.

Suddenly, I was at a small clearing. There was a cabin and smoke curling out of the chimney. I hadn't realized the chopping sound had stopped until I saw him sitting next to a wood pile.

Blue-black hair a little too shaggy to be in real fashion, and a hint of stubble across his cheeks. He was handsome, his features partway between pretty and rugged. But it wasn't his face that caught my attention. He was turned at an angle so I could see the left side of his body, the side that was a mass of scar tissue from the right side of his chest and across the top of his shoulder. I knew scars, and his was a bad one.

Even as I stared, the tug in my chest pulling me forward, two things happened almost simultaneously. I heard a twig snap behind me and the young man stood. For a moment, I thought I saw something flash behind his back. He yelled something at me and I obeyed before I'd even realized he'd told me to duck.

An ax.

He'd thrown a freaking ax at me!

Maybe it was a bit rash to jump to my feet and start cussing him out, but he had thrown an ax at my head. Well, maybe not at my head because he'd told me to duck, but he'd thrown it before I'd acted, so it was bad enough.

I was just starting to get good and riled up when I felt a sharp pain explode through the back of my head, and then everything went dark.

Chapter Six

Bram

"Seriously, Kassia?" I glared down at her. I was nearly a full foot taller than she was, but she didn't even blink.

She raised one pierced eyebrow. "What? You wanted me to let her keep going on like that? I was afraid she was going to take a swing at you."

"Did you have to knock her out though? Now we have to wait until she wakes up to talk to her."

"Talk to her?" Kassia looked at me like I'd lost my mind, and maybe I had. Her slight Korean accent thickened as her annoyance with me grew. "She saw you kill a demon, Bram. We need to get her into the cabin, and get out of here before she wakes up and calls the cops. We can't afford to get mixed up with the authorities, especially..."

Her voice trailed off but I didn't need her to finish the sentence. I knew what she'd been going to say. We didn't need any problems since we couldn't rely on back-up anymore.

"What's going on?" Fynn appeared behind her as if she'd called him, and maybe she had.

Yet another of those bonded things I'd never have. Something twisted inside me. Something new, and I shoved it aside. I had enough to deal with at the moment, not the least of which was an unconscious woman lying at my feet while a demon's corpse lay a few feet away.

And not just any woman, but a woman with one of our tattoos.

"We need to leave," Kassia said. "Burn the body, get the girl into the cabin, get out of here."

"We can't leave her here." My head jerked up. I didn't like the spike of panic that went through me at the thought of leaving her behind. I shook it off as residual feelings brought on by the fact that we'd thought we were the only ones left. It couldn't be anything else.

"What are you saying, mate?" Fynn asked. "If you killed a demon in front of her, we can't be sticking around to wait for her to wake up. Best she thinks it was a bad dream."

"She's one of us."

My statement stopped both of them. Kassia turned towards me slowly.

"Say that again."

I crouched next to the girl and gingerly touched her hand to turn her arm. Something in my gut told me to avoid touching the mark at all costs. A part of me had been hoping I'd imagined it, that it was some other kind of tattoo that I, in my grief over losing my world, had imagined to be like mine. Now, I could see it clearly and knew it for what it was. It should have been impossible, but she was Qaniss.

I heard Kassia mutter something I dimly recognized as some sort of prayer. I should've been praying too, I knew, asking Adonai for guidance. I couldn't seem to find the words though.

"Do you think that's her?" Fynn asked. "The Twelfth that Viator sent us to find?"

I shook my head. "I don't know. Viator made it sound like we were the only ones left aside from the Twelfth, but if she's here, where's her bonded?"

I glanced towards the trees, half-expecting another Qaniss to appear, to demand to know what we were doing with his or her bonded. A flash of what felt like jealousy went through me, surprising me. I hadn't been jealous of not having a bonded for years.

"Maybe dead?" Kassia said. She and Fynn looked at each other, one of those knowing looks only a bonded pair could manage.

"She should be dead then," I said, standing.

"Unless it just happened," Kassia offered.

"Or her bonded could be captured," Fynn said. "Wherever they are, they're going to be coming for her. We need to get her inside and have Lucan take a look at her."

"Agreed." I leaned down and easily picked her up. She

tensed for a moment, then relaxed against me.

I'd originally thought I'd hand her over to Fynn and take care of the demon body myself, but now that I had her in my arms, I was strangely reluctant to let her go.

"I'll take her inside. Can the two of you burn the body?"

"No problem," Kassia said.

Fynn gave me a puzzled look, and then nodded. We didn't know each other well, but I had a reputation for not being much of a people person.

As I walked towards the cabin, I looked down at the young woman in my arms. Still numb from the loss of so much, none of us as really given much thought to the task Viator had given us, to find the Twelfth. We'd come here because he'd told us where to go. I doubted any of us had consciously expected to find some random Qaniss who fit the prophecy Viator had given us, certainly not like this. If I would've thought of it, I would've assumed the Twelfth was a child, one who hadn't yet received their power, who would bond with...

I frowned. With the rest of our world gone, I didn't know how any of this would work. Then again, I'd learned years ago that Adonai rarely did things in ways that made sense.

I felt a strange tug inside me, and tried hard to ignore it. She had to be a Qaniss who'd come here with her bonded on a mission. She didn't know about our home, and she wasn't part of our mission. She and her bonded could figure out what they wanted to do next, and the rest of us would go on our way.

Except I didn't think things were going to be quite so simple.

Chapter Seven

Tempest

I heard voices as I slowly came back to consciousness, their statements fading in and out, not making any real sense.

"...it's a coincidence..."

"...you canna feel it?"

"...reaching for something..."

"...impossible..."

I tried to tune out the noise and focus on the other things that could tell me where I was, and what had happened.

First, I was laying on something. It wasn't as hard as a floor, as narrow as a couch, or as comfortable as a regular bed. That, combined with the faint smell of smoke and common sense, told me I was most likely in the cabin I'd seen. I supposed it was possible I'd been taken somewhere else, but the odds were on my side that I was right. The different voices told me the man I'd seen outside wasn't the only person in the cabin. I heard at least two male voices and two female ones. I wished they'd say something that would tell me what their intentions were.

The throbbing at the base of my skull made me think things weren't going to be simple. Then again, I didn't know why I would expect my life to be anything other than difficult.

"She's awake."

I froze. I hadn't opened my eyes, hadn't breathed any harder or moved. I'd perfected fake sleeping over the years. How had he known I was awake?

"Are you sure?" A woman's voice this time. Young, probably close to my age. "She doesn't look it."

"Trust me." The man's voice was quiet, but he had a note of authority that immediately made me think he was the leader of the group.

I heard footsteps coming closer and I decided there wasn't a point to keeping up the charade. At least I could meet whatever was coming headfirst. I opened my eyes and pushed myself up into a sitting position. A sharp pain went through my head and I felt nauseous, but I didn't let any of it show. If there was one thing I'd learned in my seventeen years, it was to never show weakness.

The young man who crouched in front of me was the same one who'd thrown the ax, though he was wearing a shirt now. His eyes were a gray so dark they looked like the kind of smoke that came from a coal fire. He was even more good-looking up close.

I didn't let any of that distract me though. I didn't know him or the people crowding around behind him. His appearance was the least of what I needed to think about.

There were ten others. I was tough, but some of these guys were big and all of them, girls included, looked like they'd seen things worse than I ever had. One guy had an eye patch and the years-old scars coming out from under it told me it was a permanent thing. At least the scar on my cheek wouldn't seem so odd around them.

"How long have you been here?" the young man asked.

That seemed like an odd question to start with. No asking my name or why I was in the woods. No explaining his insane behavior.

"You threw an ax at my head," I said the only thing I could think of. Okay, so it wasn't much better than his question, but I thought my statement was a bit more relevant.

"To kill the *deamhan*." A red-head spoke up form behind him.

"Excuse me?" I looked at each face, waiting for someone to crack a smile, to tell me I'd misunderstood the Gaelic word for *demon*, but no one did. "Who are you people?"

"I'm Bram Grimm," the young man spoke again. He pointed at each of the others as he said their names.

There was absolutely no way those were their real names. Annabella and Leigh Poe? Maybe one literary joke, sure, but not eleven of them. Something very bizarre was going on here.

And even stranger, I suddenly realized, was the pull inside

me had stopped. I no longer felt any urge to keep moving. Like I'd found whatever it was I'd been looking for.

That scared me more than the fact that I had eleven strangers standing around me.

"What happened?" I demanded. I reached behind me, certain my knife would be gone, but it was still there. I didn't pull it out, but knowing it was available helped. The guy who'd thrown the ax, Bram, seemed like the one calling the shots, so I directed my statements and questions towards him. "How did I end up in here and why does my head hurt?"

"Um, that was me."

I looked over at a thin young woman with golden skin and purple-streaked black hair.

"Sorry," she said. "You were freaking out and I thought knocking you out was the fastest way to calm you down."

"Sure," I said. "Completely understandable." Sarcasm dripped off of each word. "Not that I had a legitimate reason to be freaking out."

"She dinna realize you were one of us. Viator told us no one else had survived." The one who'd been introduced as Tady spoke up. She'd been the one who'd spoken Gaelic, and with her accent, I understood why.

"Quiet," Bram said sharply. He looked up and there was something on his face I couldn't read. "Are you really that slow?"

The girl winced and I felt bad for her. Apparently, I wasn't the only one who didn't know what was going on.

"Hey," I snapped, pulling Bram's attention back to me. "How about instead of assuming everyone here can read your mind, you actually share some information. Like what's going on and who you are."

Judging by the surprised expression on his face, he wasn't used to being talked to like that. I didn't care though. The others could treat him however they wanted. I didn't change who I was for authority figures I knew, much less some stranger who didn't look much older than me.

"What's your name?" A young man with ash blond hair and a Texas drawl asked the question.

I started to give them a false name, but then figured it couldn't hurt to say my real one. It wasn't like they could do a search on me or anything. I didn't exist anymore. "Tempest Black."

Over the years, I'd gotten a lot of comments and reactions to my unique name. Nothing, however, compared to the ten shocked expressions and the totally blank face of the young man in front of me. They looked like I'd said I was Cleopatra or Joan of Arc.

"The Dark Storm." Tady stared at me with wide eyes.

My eyebrows went up. This was getting stranger by the minute. I needed to figure out some way to get out of here, away from these crazy people. I didn't know what had brought me here, but I was suddenly sure I didn't want to stick around and find out.

"Everyone out." Bram didn't look away from me as he gave the order.

The others filed out into what I now saw was the main room of a cabin. I was lying on a bed in a side room that was barely big enough to be called an actual room. Which meant it had a door. Which was now shutting and leaving me inside with a stranger. A stranger who stared at me with an intensity that made me squirm.

I was seriously starting to regret having left Ohio.

"May I?" Bram gestured towards a space at the edge of the bed. "Crouching like this isn't exactly comfortable."

I nodded, shifting my body so my knife was more easily accessible. Bram didn't look like he'd be a pushover in a fight, but neither was I, headache or not.

"Were you born here?" he asked. His tone was conversational, light, but some sixth sense told me his question had a deeper purpose than small talk.

"No," I said. "I was born in Ohio."

"And," he hesitated for a moment, then continued, "your

parents?"

"Dead," I said flatly. "Or as well as. Are you curious or trying to figure out if you can kidnap me without anyone missing me? I'd like to know what I'm in for."

Sometimes being flat-out honest startled people into revealing more information than they normally would.

"We're orphans as well," he said. Pain flashed through his eyes, making them darken like storm clouds.

"I'm sorry." My voice softened.

I knew that expression. Being an orphan was a new thing for them. For me, I'd always been one. I'd never known either of my parents, so while it had been a sad thing when I'd been younger, in a way, it'd been better. I couldn't imagine the pain of having had parents, and then losing them. You couldn't truly miss what you'd never had.

Something clicked and I frowned. Aside from the twins, everyone else had given different last names. How could ten sets of parents just die suddenly? Maybe a couple of them were adopted, but I wasn't getting that vibe from them. Growing up in the system, I had a feel for that kind of thing, sorting out the different ways people were connected. These ones, they were all linked together somehow, but they also seemed to be paired off. Except Bram. He was one of them, but not one of them.

"Tempest?"

I shook my head, his voice bringing me out from wherever it had gone. Bram was studying me as if he could read my mind or my soul. It was a little disconcerting to say the least. At least he wasn't staring at my scar. I could tell the difference.

"I have a story to tell you," he said. "One you'll most likely not believe, but I ask that you at least hear me out." He spoke matter-of-factly.

"Will it explain why you and your buddies are acting so weird?" I asked.

"It will."

"All right," I said. "But you stay over there. You try to touch me or come any closer, we're going to have a problem."

The corner of Bram's mouth twitched, and I caught a hint of surprise in his expression. He must not smile much, I thought.

"Agreed," he said. "I won't try to touch you or move any closer. May I turn so I'm facing you?"

I liked that he asked so I nodded. It had nothing to do with the fact that I thought he was cute. Attraction was the last thing on my mind.

"You seem like the kind of person who can tell when someone is lying."

"Most of the time," I said warily. How had he figured that?

"Then I want you to be able to see me clearly," he said. "Because what I'm about to tell you isn't going to be easy for you to hear, or believe."

Now my curiosity was overwhelming my concern. What in the world had I stumbled into?

He was silent for nearly a full minute before he started to speak. "I've never had to explain this before. I'm not entirely sure where to start."

His tone suggested being at a loss wasn't something he experienced often, and it would've amused me if I hadn't been anticipating hearing something very strange.

"No matter where I start, it's going to sound crazy," he said. He looked down at his hands, his thumb rubbing against a spot on the inside of his right wrist. "So I suppose I'll start here." He turned his hand towards me.

There, on his wrist, the spot he'd been rubbing, was a Celtic cross. It was identical in size and shape to the one I had. In the same place.

"What a strange coincidence." My voice sounded a little shaky. That kind of cross wasn't exactly uncommon, but it wasn't very common either, and the placement, while not totally unique, did make it strange for the exact same design.

He shook his head. "It's not a coincidence." He gestured towards the door. "Each one of us has the same tattoo in the same place. It's the mark of who we are. What we are."

My chest felt tight and I could feel my pulse increasing. That wasn't possible. The odds were too unlikely.

He continued, "We're known by many names. Shadow Riders, Star Children, *Nadzirateli*, *y Gwylwyr, Los Vigilantes, csillag lovasok*." The foreign languages rolled off his tongue. "Most commonly, including here, we're called Star Riders. Some places, we're mistaken for angels or ghosts. In the past, extra terrestrials or gods. We call ourselves Qaniss."

He pronounced it *KAW-nis*, and I could almost see the word in my head even though I knew I'd never heard it before.

I leaned back against the wall, suddenly light-headed.

"No matter what name we're given, we have one job." He kept his eyes on my face when he said it. "We're demon hunters."

"Uh-huh." I stared at him. He wasn't lying. At least not in the sense that he knew what he was saying was crazy.

He gave me a wry smile. "I know how this sounds."

"I'm not sure you do," I countered. How in the world had I managed to find a group of crazy people out in the middle of nowhere?

"Just wait," he said. "It's about to get even weirder."

I cursed under my breath. That wasn't possible, was it?

"I'm not going to tell you everything at once," he said. "It'll be too much. Where we came from, how we're here, all of that I'll tell you in due time, but there is at least one other thing you need to know."

"Okay," I said it slowly, unsure if I wanted to know what was coming next. What I did know was he was talking as if I was going to be around long enough for him to gradually tell me his entire story.

"You're one of us too."

Oh, yeah, he was nuts. Completely bug-nuts.

"We were sent here to find you," he said. "To fulfill a prophecy none of us had ever really taken seriously until you told us your name."

A prophecy. Right. This kept getting better and better.

"Growing up, we'd always heard the prophecy of the Twelve. The final Star Riders, the final Qaniss. They would be the ones left at the end of time to decide the balance between good and evil, to be the last defense against the powers of dark." He shook his head and his hair fell in front of his eyes. He brushed at it with an impatient gesture. "I don't know if any of us really believed it. It was the future, something far off that generations after generations wouldn't have to worry about."

I wanted to interrupt him, tell him none of this made sense. The problem was, the tug was back. It wasn't pulling me towards something, not exactly, but I couldn't exactly explain it either. It was like something deep in my gut was telling me to believe him, no matter how crazy it sounded.

"Then, a couple days ago, the eleven of us were told the full prophecy and sent here to find the last one, the last member of the Twelve."

"And you think that's me," I said. "Because of this?" I held up my wrist. "It's a tattoo I got on a whim."

"Not on a whim," he said. His voice was calm. "Adonai spoke to you."

Oh great, we were going to there. "Look, Bram, I don't know what you think, but it's just a tattoo. I have another one." I shrugged off my jacket and tugged on the collar of my shirt. "See?"

His face went pale. "It can't be."

Okay, not the reaction I'd expected.

"Was your mother's name Susanna?"

That wasn't possible. "How did you know that?" I could barely get the question out.

"I didn't really believe it." He seemed to be talking to himself rather than me. "I'd always thought these things were stories told to bolster confidence, give the people hope."

"Are you going to clue me in or keep muttering to yourself?" I asked, my voice sharp.

He looked up at me, something unreadable in his eyes.

"*The Dark Storm with lost founder's power shall appear in the last hour. Trust shall make the way clear. The Twelve will rise and all will fear. From time's end to end, they shall fight, either for darkness or for light.*'"

The hair on my arms stood on end.

"How did you know my mother's name?" I heard my voice shaking and hated myself for it, but I couldn't stop it. That gut feeling I had was getting stronger, and I didn't like it. This wasn't some fight or flight reaction or something like that. No, this was a part of me I'd never wanted to acknowledge. A part of me thought maybe there was something to the stories I'd heard the few times my house parents dragged me to church.

"Adonai, help me," he murmured. He reached out like he was going to touch me and I jerked my arm away. "Sorry."

"You need to start talking," I said. My heart was racing and the pain in my head had doubled. "Otherwise, I'm leaving and going straight to the cops."

The look he gave me said he knew I wasn't going anywhere near a police station. "You're going to think I'm crazy."

"Too late," I retorted.

"All right then." He folded his hands on his lap. "Here it goes."

Chapter Eight

Bram

How was I supposed to explain something every Qaniss was taught from birth? Immersed in until it was a part of who we were?

I took a deep breath and dove right in. "When Adonai – God, Elohim, Elyon, Jehovah, whatever you want to call Him – created the world, He gave Adam and Eve free will. He also established facts scientists would eventually come to call laws. Among those laws is one stating every action–"

"Will have an equal and opposite reaction," she interrupted. "I took science in school. I just want to know what this has to do with you knowing my mom's name and why you think I'm some demon hunting freak."

I scowled at her description of us, but tried to put myself in her shoes. She had clearly been alone for a long time and I, of all people, understood what it was like to be Qaniss and alone. And I had at least known what I was.

I kept my voice calm and even. "You need to hear this to understand the rest."

She gave me a skeptical look, but let me continue.

"I don't know exactly how it all works, but I'm going to explain it the way it was explained to me as a child," I said.

"When a person exercises their free will, the opposite choice creates, for the lack of a better word, a bubble. Most of the time, that bubble is absorbed back into the world because the opposite choice doesn't have long-reaching effects. For example, you're out shopping and you choose a particular brand of soap. The consequences of choosing something else bubble out around you, but since the next steps you take end up being the same, the bubbles are brought back into your timeline and nothing happens."

She didn't look like she believed me, but at least she appeared to be following what I was saying.

"Some choices, however, are important enough, the world can't go back to the way it was, and the bubble breaks off, creating a new world, one that picks up from the point of that decision."

"You're talking about parallel worlds," she said. "Like some other place where the Titanic didn't sink so we're all in flying cars or something, or Hitler was killed before World War II and the Holocaust never happened."

I nodded, relieved she at least grasped it on an intellectual level. I knew she hadn't accepted it as truth, but one step at a time. "There are tens of thousands of parallel worlds. Some very similar, but with slight differences that kept them from being reintegrated into the original world."

"And those worlds have spin-off worlds and so on, right?" She rolled her eyes.

"No." I ignored the attitude even as I found myself respecting it. This girl was tough. "Only the choices on the original world create new ones." A pang went through me as I realized something for the first time. "And now that the original world is...done, no new ones will be made."

"What does that mean?"

"The Qaniss come – came – from the original world and we have the ability to travel between worlds. Only those with Qaniss blood have the ability." I paused, and then added, "As well as a handful of angels who had been created different so they could carry messages into all the worlds."

She shook her head. "Do you have any idea how insane you sound?"

"Tempest."

I didn't let myself think about how her name made the power inside me pulse. That was definitely a conversation to have at another time. Maybe.

"There is a world where rogue Qaniss intermarried and genetic manipulation gave people wings like ours to fly over their poisoned grass. I've personally seen a world where a comet hit North America, and the survivors are underground, waiting to emerge decades from now. A place where a simple refusal to follow God's commands far in the past allowed people to develop the ability to manipulate the world around them in a way they call magic. And dragons."

"Dragons?"

"Well, a dragon, singular, but it existed."

She shook her head again. "That's not possible. Scientists propose the theory of parallel worlds, but not the way you're talking about."

"This is one."

"Excuse me?"

"This isn't the original world. That world is gone." I pushed back the pain. "We're all that's left."

"Then I can't be one of you," she said. "Because I was born here. Believe me, I heard the story enough growing up. The social workers loved telling it to potential parents. How my mom died giving birth to me, how she barely had the strength to name me."

"And she named you Tempest Black," I said. "The Dark Storm."

"Stop with that," she snapped, eyes flashing.

Something inside me twisted and I didn't like it. I didn't want to feel anything for her.

"Tell me how you know my mom's name," she demanded.

She deserved to know. "You may have been born here, but

you're not from here. You and your mother came from my world."

"And you just happen to know that?" she asked.

"The first Qaniss had a daughter named Susanna. She was six months pregnant when she vanished. Legend has it, the demons took her to another world, but no one knew how to get her back. Hundreds of years passed, and everyone assumes she died long ago, ending the line as well." I fought to keep my voice steady. She didn't need to know what this meant for me personally, or about the prophecy that had been made regarding that particular descendant.

"Well, I'm not hundreds of years old," she said.

I shook my head as I realized what must've happened. "Time moves differently in some of the more...demonic realms. I believe Susanna was held there and escaped to here in time to give birth to you. You are the grand-daughter of the original Qaniss, and his power flows through your veins." I pointed towards the tattoo on her collarbones. "And that proves it."

"How?"

"Because your grandfather was William Shakespeare."

When she passed out, I wondered if maybe I should've eased her into that particular revelation. There was a reason I'd never been involved in missions that required diplomacy or people skills. I didn't have either.

"Lucan!" I called as I stood.

He opened the door immediately, knife in hand, body tense and ready for a fight. It took him less time to assess the situation than it would have for me to explain it, and he reacted at once.

I stepped aside as he went down on a knee so he could better examine her and it was harder than I wanted to admit to move even a short distance away from her.

"How hard did Kassia hit her?" he asked as he pressed his fingers against the side of her head.

"I don't know." I crossed my arms, then uncrossed them, unsure what to do with my hands. "Is she okay?"

"What happened?"

"We were talking and she passed out." I hesitated, and then added, "I might've told her about who we were...and where we were from."

The only indication I had he'd even heard me was a minute pause, so small no one but a Qaniss could've seen it. He ran his hands along her arms, and then down over her torso. A flash of jealousy went through me and I frowned. I had no right to feel jealous. I had no right to feel anything. She was a stranger to me. Part of our mission, but that was all.

"Make sure she's okay and come out. We have to decide

what to do now." I didn't wait for him to respond since I knew he wouldn't. He was focused on his work.

Everyone was waiting for me in the main area, all crammed together. The living room would've been comfortable with a group half our size, but we'd shared tighter quarters than this so none of us thought anything of it. All eyes turned towards me when I walked in.

"Is the lass all right?" Tady asked. "Why did ye call Lucan in?"

"She passed out," I said. I glanced at Kassia. "Not entirely uncommon with a head injury."

"And how should I have handled it?" she asked mildly. "She wasn't exactly being reasonable."

"I told her," I said.

"How much?" Annabella asked.

"Enough."

I walked over to the fireplace and held out my hands to the warmth. The back room was cool though I was pretty sure my chill had nothing to do with the temperature. I considered seeing if we had a spare blanket somewhere for Tempest, but pushed the thought aside. Her comfort shouldn't have been my primary concern. I didn't want it to be.

The door opened and I turned as Lucan came out of the room. "How is she?"

"I think it's mostly exhaustion and dehydration," he said. "That, plus Kassia's little tap on the head and the shock of everything was too much for her." His Texas accent, while usually very faint, had thickened and the look in his dark eyes was one of worry.

"What is it?" Leigh asked. "There's something else, isn't there?"

"She has...scars." Lucan looked vaguely ill.

"We all have scars," Annabella said with a shrug.

"She's not...she wasn't raised like us," Lucan countered. "One cut on her shoulder's fairly new. So are the bruises on her face, and some on her ribs."

"The scar on her face isn't new," Tady said.

"No," Lucan agreed. "It's not. And neither are the ones on her back and shoulders. Ones that look like cigarette burns and whip marks." He glanced at me. "Someone hurt her when she was younger. Badly."

My stomach clenched and I felt sick. Abusing anyone made me angry, but the thought of someone doing that to Tempest was like a fist in the stomach.

I pushed my feelings aside as best I could. This wasn't the time or the place. "We need to decide what we're going to do with her."

"Do with her?" Tady didn't seem to like my choice of

words. "She's a person, Bram."

"She's not just a person," I said. "She's the Twelfth. The one we were sent to find. And she has no clue who we are or what we do." I glanced at the door. "I don't even think she follows Adonai."

"That does complicate things," Annabella said.

"That's putting it mildly," Emilia muttered as she signed to Harrison.

I agreed with them both, but couldn't express my doubts. I had to stay focused, and come up with a plan. But first, there was one other thing I needed to tell them.

"The prophecy," I began. "It refers to her as the Dark Storm." The others nodded. They'd all heard that part before.

"Her name does seem to fit," Kassia said.

"There's more to her name than that," I said. "Tempest. As in *The Tempest*."

Fynn got it first. "No way."

"The first line says she'll have 'lost founder's power.'" I turned back to the fire so they couldn't see my face. "Her mother's name was Susanna."

"That's impossible, Bram," Annabella said. "Susanna Shakespeare disappeared from our world centuries ago. She's long dead, and her child with her."

"I don't think so." I had to chose my words carefully. "She

has 'To thine own self be true' tattooed across her collarbones."

"All that means is she's a fan of his works," Annabella argued. "You're taking a lot on faith that she's even one of us. We've seen people on hundreds of worlds where people have cross tattoos. Even some where they wear them on their wrists like we do."

"I can feel her, Annabella," I snapped. I knew they were staring at me now, but I stayed turned away.

"No one bonds after the age of twelve," Lucan said softly. "Even if she was supposed to be yours, the bond would be dead after seven years. Especially since you..." His voice trailed off but he didn't have to finish his sentence. Everyone knew what he was going to say.

"I can't explain it," I said. That wasn't entirely true, since I knew something they didn't, but that was none of their business. "All I know is, my power is calling to hers."

"She can't have power," Emilia said. "Even if she has the tattoo, there was no one here to do the ritual. It's only ink."

"It makes a sort of sense."

I turned to look at Tady, surprised by her sudden support.

She shrugged. "Why else would Adonai send us eleven to find a twelfth? Five pairs and one who never bonded? It makes sense the twelfth would complete the group."

There was silence for a moment and then Fynn spoke, "Out

of the mouths of babes."

"Fynn!" Tady protested and I saw Bair shoot the other man a dirty look.

Fynn grinned as Kassia rolled her eyes. "I was referring to her age."

"That's not any better." Tady scowled.

"Look, Bram, this is all well and good if this girl is who you're saying she is." Annabella brought the conversation back around. "But it's not going to do us any good if we can't get her to believe us. If you're right, you need to bond with her, and the sooner the better. If it even works at all."

It would work. I could feel it. The power inside me was thrumming, and it felt like every cell in my body was vibrating. It hadn't been like that since right after it had been given to me, before I'd learned to contain it. If it had only been about the power, I would've walked back into the room and done the ritual the moment Tempest woke up. But there was something else at stake here, and I wasn't willing to risk it.

"We can't force her into this," I said. "It has to be her choice."

Kassia rolled her eyes. "It's in her blood, Bram. And if she is who you say she is, it's more in her blood than any of ours. One generation removed from an original. None of us can say that."

"Trying to bond after the age of twelve has never been done," I said firmly. "We don't know what could happen, and I'm not going to make that choice for her."

"A single Qaniss has also never been able to handle the power alone, but you have," Grady reminded me quietly. "None of this is exactly in the realm of normal."

"The longer we stay here, the more danger other worlds will be in," Annabella said. "There are demons out there right now, taking advantage of the situation, destroying everything our people built. Everything we sacrificed and died for. We don't have time to wait for her to come around."

"Annabella." Leigh's voice was soft, but it immediately stopped whatever else her sister had been going to say. "Adonai never forces His will on anyone. We always have a choice. Even the prophecy says it." She looked around at each one of us. "We had a choice to come here. Who are we to take away hers?"

The silence following Leigh's statement spoke volumes. She'd ended the argument, no doubt about it, and I was going to get what I wanted. Time. And while I did believe it should be Tempest's choice, there was another reason I wanted to wait. A purely selfish one.

I covered my wrist with my hand, pressing my palm against the throbbing tattoo. Until I could figure out what to do

about the other prophecy, I couldn't forge a bond with
Tempest.

For the first time in my life, I wished my father was here to
offer advice. Tears burned at my eyelids and I pushed them
back. I wouldn't show weakness. I had to be strong. It was my
place, my duty.

"We'll take turns sitting with her," I said. "We're going to
let her choose her path, but we need to make sure she
understands all of the consequences of her choice. We can't let
her run away."

"I'll take first watch," Lucan offered.

I nodded at him. "Let's all get some rest. I have a feeling
we're going to be in for a long couple days ahead."

If I'd known what was coming, I might've amended my
statement to something more emphatic. But I wasn't a Seer.
The future was just as dark to me as it was to everyone else.
The only thing I did know for certain about my future was that,
for good or bad, Tempest Black would play a part.

Chapter Nine

Tempest

When I woke up, it was night, and the only light in the room came from the moon outside. The small, lone window didn't have curtains. The shadowed darkness was disorienting at first and I kept myself still to allow for time to adjust.

I still didn't know why I was here. The real reason, since there was no way what I remembered from my previous conversation could have been true. A part of me even wondered if I'd dreamed it. After all, no sane person would actually believe any of what that guy had told me.

A young man was sitting in a chair in the far corner a few feet from the bottom corner of the bed. He looked like he was my age, maybe a bit younger. About average height and lean, but from what I could see, his arms were firmly muscled. I doubted he'd be easy to take out.

I looked over at the door, wondering if I could get to it before he woke up.

I flinched as the door opened with a faint creak. A figure filled the doorway and, for a moment, panic flared, sharp and bright, as a memory tried to force its way forward. Then a voice came from the figure and, despite who it belonged to, it chased away the panic.

Or maybe it was because of who the voice belonged to.

I frowned, unsure where the thought had come from and not liking it.

"Fynn," the man spoke again. "Doesn't do any good to be on watch if you fall asleep."

I looked over at the man in the chair. He was awake now, and even in the dim lighting, I could see the flush on his cheeks. He darted a glance at me and I saw a pair of baby blue eyes with a sheepish expression.

"I'll take over."

Fynn stood, nodded at the guy in doorway and stepped out into the main room. The man from before – Bram, like *Dracula* – came inside and closed the door behind him. He went to the chair and sat down, loosely clasping his hands in front of him so I could see he didn't have a weapon.

"You guys are going to take turns watching me so I don't escape?" I pushed myself up in a sitting position. My head felt better, but I still got a swift stab of pain through my temple from moving too fast. That didn't bode well for me being able to defend myself. "Why not tie me up? Or maybe you like watching me sleep. Which is kinda creepy, just so you know."

"You're not a prisoner, Tempest." Bram sounded tired and I wondered if he'd gotten any sleep himself.

"Then I can walk out of here right now?" I swung my legs

over the edge of the bed as if I intended to get up.

"You could," he said. "If you wanted to walk down a mountain in the dark and cold."

His face was shadowed and his voice flat, but I got the impression that my intentions amused him.

I sighed. He was right. If they'd been hurting me, I would've risked it, but it seemed more prudent to wait at least until it was light. And if I got some answers in the meantime, all the better. He obviously knew too much about me.

"I know you don't believe me," he said. "Not on a conscious level, but I think somewhere, deep inside you, you know I'm telling the truth."

I shook my head even though I knew he was right. That tug I'd had for weeks had turned into some sort of intuition. I'd always had a good sense about people and it seemed to be even stronger when it came to these people, to this man in particular. And it was telling me to believe him.

"Tempest." His voice softened. "I've grown up knowing this all my life, was raised Qaniss. I've traveled the spaces between, seen with my own eyes worlds beyond imagination. And even I sometimes have a hard time believing it myself."

"What do you want?" I made my voice as hard as I could.

He leaned forward and held out his hand. His fingers were long and strong-looking. A shaft of moonlight cut across his skin and I could see dozens of small, white scars covering his palm and fingers. My gaze was drawn to the tattoo on his wrist, and I had the sudden urge to touch it.

"When a Qaniss is ready to receive the power needed to kill demons and travel between worlds, he or she receives this tattoo. It's more than ink. It's imbued with power that can't be explained."

I put my hand over my own mark. "It's only a tattoo. I got it when I was ten to piss off my foster mom."

"Ten?"

Something about the way Bram said the word made me sit forward. I narrowed my eyes. "Yeah, why?"

"How old are you?"

I blinked. "Seventeen."

Bram's face paled, and I saw myriad emotions flicker across his eyes before a mask slammed down into place. Whatever had just happened, he wasn't going to share.

"I'm going to ask you to do something," he said. "Only one thing. And if you still don't believe me, when the sun comes up, I'll walk you down the mountain myself."

I gave him a skeptical look.

"I'm not going to hurt you," he said.

"Like you could," I scoffed. "I can take care of myself."

"I believe you."

I wanted to bristle against his remark, but he'd said it so matter-of-factly that I couldn't get annoyed.

"All I want you to do is put your fingers on my tattoo. That's all."

Touch his wrist. I supposed he could try to grab me while my hand was there, but it didn't really make sense. There'd be a million other ways to get to me if he wanted to hurt me. This would've been a dumb ruse. I started to stretch out my left hand.

"With your right hand, please."

As I shifted my weight so I could reach out with my right hand, I saw the muscles in his arm tense. It wasn't like the kind of tension that came before a sudden movement. More like he was preparing to feel something he wasn't sure he could handle.

"Your first two fingers. Put them on the cross."

The instant my skin touched his, a jolt of something went through me. It didn't hurt, not exactly, but I felt like I'd touched one of those low-current electrical fences. The hairs on my arm stood up as every cell in my body lit up like a Christmas tree. I felt like I was glowing, like I could take on an army, run down the mountain in a snowstorm...

Bram jerked his arm back, breaking the connection. His breathing was harsh and ragged, like he'd run a marathon.

"What–?" I gasped. "What was that?" I stared at my fingers. They were still tingling.

"That," Bram said. "Is the power Adonai gave to the Qaniss."

I stared at him, but he wasn't looking at me. I frowned. I wanted to know what he was thinking, what he'd felt. Obviously, it had been something, but had it been the same thing I'd felt? I put my fingers against my own tattoo. There was no jolt or intense sensation, but I could feel something there below the surface, like something was there, waiting to be released.

I didn't believe him. I couldn't. It simply wasn't possible. But there wasn't any logical explanation for what I'd felt, what I was still feeling.

And then I saw them.

Wings.

He had wings.

Huge, beautiful wings with feathers the glossy blue-black of a crow, streaked with the same slate gray as his eyes. They were stretched out behind him, the tips touching each side of the room.

"You...you..." I had the idea it was probably rude of me to be staring at them but I couldn't make myself stop.

Bram must've figured out what I was looking at because

the wings started to fold in, and then they disappeared, making me wonder if they'd even been there at all. There was absolutely no way he could have wings.

"Yeah, those are real."

I met his eyes and they were clear. No deceit. He wasn't joking, making fun of me or crazy. He was dead serious.

"Adonai gave us a little something extra to help us in the fight." The wings appeared again, fluttering a bit. "All of us get them when we receive Adonai's power."

"And they disappear?" I was impressed I managed a full question.

He shrugged and they moved with his shoulders. "Don't ask me how. Some Qaniss spend their lives trying to figure it out. No one ever has. We pull them in and when they touch our backs, they...disappear."

I had to be dreaming. That was the only logical explanation. Right? But, no. I knew I was awake. And I knew I was seeing what I was seeing. I'd always made it a point not to lie to myself, and I didn't plan on starting now.

I had a choice to make then. I could walk away, pretend like the sixth sense I'd always relied on wasn't telling me to stay, pretend none of this had really happened, or I could accept that I needed to stay. And even if I thought about it logically, I didn't have another explanation for what I'd seen. It came down to the whole 'when you eliminate the impossible...' way of looking at things. A supernatural presence wasn't something I considered completely impossible, which meant that, however unlikely I found the story, until a better explanation came along, I was going to have to go with what I had.

"All right," I said finally. "What's next?"

He looked at me now, surprise on his face. "That's it? You get zapped with Adonai's power, see my wings, and you just ask what's next?"

I shrugged. "Would you prefer I blather on about something completely irrelevant, or ask questions I know you can't answer?"

The corner of his mouth twitched as if he was trying not to laugh. "No, I suppose not."

"Then what's next?"

He stood and looked out the window. "It's still a couple hours until dawn. We'll want to wait until then to start training."

"Training?"

He nodded. "We are faster and stronger than a normal human, but we still need to train. We don't kill demons with wit."

"No, you kill them with axes."

I caught an actual glimpse of a smile this time, and it made something low in my stomach twist. I wasn't sure I liked it, but I didn't exactly dislike it either.

"We do kill them with axes. Axes, knives, arrows, guns..." He turned back towards me. "But it's not really the weapon that kills them. A regular human could shoot a demon a hundred times and it wouldn't even be phased." He gestured towards the cross. "We imbue the weapons with power. It allows us to make lethal blows." His eyes sparkled. "Like an ax to the head."

I raised an eyebrow. "Maybe we should start with what a demon looks like. I wouldn't want to accidentally kill an endangered species or something."

He laughed, then looked surprised that he had. It had been brief, barely a sound, but I got the impression it had been a while since he'd laughed. "That might be a good place to start."

"You haven't trained anyone before, have you?" I was starting to get a crick in my neck from looking up at him, but I didn't want to take my eyes off of him either. I told myself it was because I didn't entirely trust him, but I knew that wasn't exactly true.

"No," he said. "I'm a hunter, not a trainer." His expression fell. "But there isn't anyone else, so I suppose you're stuck with me."

"There's ten other people out there who could do it if you don't want to." I was trying for nonchalant, but his head came up sharply at my suggestion, his eyes flashing.

"We'll start at dawn." He walked over to the door. "I suggest you try to get some sleep. I'm not easing you into this."

He closed the door behind him before I could respond.

"What was that all about?" I muttered as I stretched back out on the bed. I knew there was a lot to learn, and a lot Bram hadn't told me about what I was and what I was supposed to do, but my intuition said there was something else going on, something Bram didn't want me to know about.

I sighed. There was no way I was going to get any sleep tonight. My head was far too busy.

Chapter Ten

Bram

I could still feel her fingers on my wrist. The power inside me was writhing beneath my skin, and I felt like every cell in my body was about to explode. I ran a hand through my hair as I stepped around the sleeping bodies of the others. My hands were shaking, and I knew if I didn't get outside, the power was going to start leaking out and it would wake the others.

I sighed as the cool air hit my face. I hadn't felt this out of control since that day seven years ago when I'd first taken the tattoo. That day, the power had hit me so hard I'd thought I was going to die. Everyone had thought I was going to die. No one had ever been able to explain why I hadn't. Now, I thought I understood.

It had been her, even then. I hadn't asked the specific date she'd gotten her tattoo, but I hadn't needed to. She'd been ten, and that was enough to make me believe. Even though no bond had been forged, no power shared, I knew the day I'd stood before the Council and declared my intent, she'd been there, in her world, taking the same mark. A link had been made, a link that had gone through the spaces between to find my other half...

I shook my head. I didn't want to think about that. Until

she was ready, there was no point in me even considering bonding with her. She wouldn't be able to handle it. At the moment, I wasn't entirely sure I could either.

I looked up as I took another deep breath. I needed to get out of here.

I spread my wings, shaking them out as I stretched them to their full six and a half feet. I could feel every inch of them humming with power.

I'd told Tempest it was too dark and cold for her to try to make her way down the mountain, but that wouldn't have been true if she'd been a Qaniss. Or at least, one with power. I didn't know how much her senses were heightened as she was, and I wasn't going to take a chance with her. Myself, I could see fine in the moonlight, and I wasn't even chilled.

I started off at a slow jog, but that didn't last long. I had too much energy, too much power humming through my body. Before I'd gone more than a couple yards away from the cabin, I broke into a run. A sense of relief rushed through me as I let the power go, fed it into my legs and feet. We were usually fast enough we didn't use our power for things like running, but tonight, I needed it.

My feet flew over the rocky ground, automatically finding the safest places to land for the split second they needed to push off again. There was no burn, no strain of muscle. The trees went by in a blur, the shadows of their leaves mere streaks in my vision. I felt the terrain sloping downward and stepped off the path, curving back up so I was going around the mountain rather than down it. Branches whipped against my arms and face, sharp, quick stings that vanished almost as quickly as they came. I barely registered them, enjoying the challenge of cutting around trees and leaping over rocks.

As I reached an edge, I jumped without a second thought and my wings caught me. I soared across a canyon, giving my legs a rest while I worked my wings. I flew for miles before turning around again. I landed easily, not missing a step as I went from flying to running, instinctively tucking my wings back in.

I didn't stop until the sun started to rise and my lungs began to burn. I skidded to a stop in a grassy clearing less than half a mile from the cabin. I forced myself to take slow, deep breaths as I moved and stretched, letting my muscles cool down.

I pushed my sweaty hair out of my face, grimacing at the feel of the wet strands. I needed a haircut soon or I was going to have to start tying it back to fight. Back home, I'd visited Summer Novak, a childhood friend of my mother's, every few weeks for a trim. I supposed I could ask one of the others to do it. Leigh had done Lucan's hair a couple days ago. I had the errant thought that maybe Tempest could do it for me, but I immediately pushed it aside. It was going to be hard enough touching her when we trained. I was going to have to be extra careful not to do it casually. Direct contact on the tattoo had been intense, but the thought alone of a casual touch was enough to make my power flare, and my heart twist.

It was almost time for me to head back. The others would be waking up soon and I didn't want them to worry. First, however, I needed to clean off. There was a bathroom in the cabin, and the water managed to get decently hot for a couple minutes, but I thought something cold might be better. I needed to focus, and that would be the best way to do it.

Training would be tough, but resisting the urge to bond with her was going to be worse. I could feel it, the pull I'd been trying to ignore. The power inside me was calling to hers, and I knew it would only get worse the longer I waited.

I sighed and jogged down to a stream I'd seen a few minutes ago. It was October and I could smell snow in the air. The water was going to be cold, but I didn't even hesitate to strip off my shirt when I got to the bank. I tossed it aside, kicked off my shoes and waded in. A thousand needles of ice pricked my skin, but I knew taking it slow would only make it worse. I held my breath, steeled myself and dropped in.

It took my breath away, but as I stood up, it was worth it.

One of the downsides to always running hotter than a regular person was Qaniss were rarely able to appreciate feeling cool. Now, as a gust of wind came down from the mountain, for the first time in years, goosebumps broke out across my flesh.

I opened my wings and water dripped off of them as if they'd been dunked too. I stepped out of the stream and shook my hair, sending drops of water flying everywhere. I squeezed as much water as possible from my pants – which wasn't very much since the heavy material was specifically fitted to me, which meant there wasn't a lot of give – then pulled my shoes back on. The wind had dried a lot of the water from my skin, but my hair and wings were still wet enough that the shoulders and back of my shirt were soaked almost immediately after I pulled it on.

I jogged down to the cabin, letting my body heat rise to normal again. The others would be awake soon and I knew we were going to have to start discussing what we were going to do next. Adonai had sent us here to find Tempest and had given us time to grieve. The presence of a demon when Tempest had shown up told me our brief reprieve was over. We needed to start planning our next move. Everything we had known had changed and how our people had done things for thousands of years would no longer work. We could no longer rely on the Council for guidance. It was up to us now.

Twenty minutes later, I'd told the others as much. None of us were children. Even Tady, the youngest of us at sixteen, was virtually an adult by Qaniss standards. The problem was, we were all warriors. We could survive in the wilderness for extended periods of time, find food and water in obscure places, knew how to apply field dressings and use almost anything as a weapon, but there were things we'd always taken for granted because the Council made sure the entire community cared for each other.

Case in point, none of us knew how to cook. Not real food anyway. We had the usual dried meat, fruit and nuts, but we'd finished our bread and anything fresh shortly after arriving. We needed provisions. And, of course, there were our clothes. We couldn't afford to draw attention to ourselves, and the way we looked now wouldn't exactly be unnoticeable.

"Annabella and Grady, I want the two of you hunting. See if you can get us a deer or something like that. Leigh and Lucan, medical supplies. Whatever you can find." I looked over at Emilia and Harrison. "You two are going for whatever food you can buy. Salt so we can preserve the meat. Jugs to store water. If you can, buy some fresh fruit or vegetables. Who knows how long it'll be until we can get those again. Whatever canned foods you can get." Tady and Bair were next. "Clothes. We need to know if there's anything on this world that's similar to what we use for our gear." Kassia and Fynn were already waiting expectantly. "You're on weapons detail. The more we have, the better."

"There's only so much we can take with us when we travel, Bram." Annabella gave me a shrewd look, and I watched her put it together. "We're going to leave some of it here."

I nodded. "We no longer have a...base of operations." The faces in front of me were carefully blank, but I saw a flicker of pain cross Tady's eyes. I continued, "We can't return for reinforcements, for healing, supplies of any kind. We need to set up caches in each world. Food, medicine, clothes and weapons. We don't know how long Adonai wants us to do this, so we need to be prepared."

Annabella nodded. "That's a good idea."

"What are you going to be doing?" Fynn asked.

"Training her." I jerked my head back towards the still-closed door behind me. I hadn't checked in to see if she was sleeping, but I knew she hadn't left. I could feel her. My power pulling me towards her.

"Maybe we should ask her about this world," Lucan suggested. "It is her home, after all. She'd know if there was anything we'd need to know."

"And if the currency the Council gave us for our last mission will work here," Leigh finished.

"I'll go." Annabella took a step forward and I automatically moved between her and the door. Her coal black eyes glittered dangerously. "Move out of my way, Bram."

I'd been hoping it wouldn't come to this. Out of the ten, Annabella was the only one who'd challenge my authority, and I'd hoped her sister and her bonded would be able to keep her in check. I kept my voice even. "I'll talk to her."

I saw Grady step up behind Annabella. I could see the reluctance on his face and knew that even though he had no problems with me being in charge, he was bound to Annabella and would stand at her side should things get violent.

"I don't remember anyone putting you in charge." Her hand twitched, but she didn't actually reach for the dagger at her waist.

I squared my shoulders and looked down at her. She was tall, nearly six feet, but I still had a good five inches on her and I needed her to feel every one. I'd told myself I'd never say these words, but if I didn't now, it would eventually come to us taking sides, and we didn't need that.

"'The king's name is a tower of strength,'" I quoted the original founder, the beginnings of the oath nearly sticking in my mouth.

Out of the corners of my eyes, I saw the others stiffen, felt their surprise. Annabella's mouth tightened and her hand curled into a fist. I'd started it and I needed to finish it, or things were going to get very complicated.

I'd been only six when my father had taken the oath to lead our people, but I remembered every word. He'd made me recite them in the hopes I'd succeed him when he passed. I'd never wanted it, but I knew it was my responsibility now, and I continued, "I am Bram Robert Grimm, only living descendant of Wilhelm Grimm, the oldest of the founding families. Eldest living descendant of Mary Shelly and Robert Frost. Only son of the Council leader, Abraham Jakob Grimm. Eldest of the surviving Qaniss. This is my birthright."

Technically, the claim that Wilhelm Grimm was the oldest of the founders wasn't entirely true anymore, but I didn't think Annabella would take too kindly to the reminder that the only person who really had the authority to challenge me was someone who, up until yesterday, hadn't even known what she was.

"Annabella," Grady spoke in a low voice. "It is his right."

For a moment, I thought she was going to argue, but she didn't. Instead, she gave me a curt nod and took a step back. The tension in the room eased.

"I'll talk to her," I said.

"Her has a name." Tempest's wry voice came from behind me.

I turned to see her standing in the doorway. I hadn't even heard the door open.

She crossed her arms and leaned against the doorframe. "What do you need to talk to me about?"

"Supplies," I said. "We need to know where to go and if the money we have is valid here."

Emilia stepped forward with a few bills in her hand. "It's usually about fifty-fifty whether or not our money will work. It generally depends at what time the parallel world was created."

Tempest nodded as she accepted the money and began to examine it. "Right, like if a world was created before the Civil War, Abraham Lincoln might not be on the five dollar bill because something could've happened in that world to prevent him from becoming President."

"She catches on quick," Kassia said.

"Again," Tempest said mildly. "She has a name."

Kassia grinned. "All right, Tempest Black, daughter of Susanna, only living descendant of William Shakespeare. You've got a name."

Tempest's face paled, then flooded with color, making the jagged scar on her face stand out. "Just Tempest is fine," she muttered.

"So, just Tempest, do the bills pass inspection?" Fynn

asked.

"They'll work," she said. "But I wouldn't use anything bigger than a ten. Some stores use a special pen to see if bills twenty and higher are fake. I don't know if the paper and ink you guys used would pass." She turned to me. "Does this mean we're training while they're all out shopping?"

"We are," I said. "Give Tady your measurements. They're doing a clothes run."

Tempest's eyes darkened. "I can take care of my own clothes, thank you very much."

I raised an eyebrow. "Not if you're training all day."

She glared at me. "Let's get one thing straight. Even if I do believe you about who I am, and I agree to let you train me to kill demons, you're not my boss. You don't get to tell me what to do."

Heat rose in my face and my temper flared. With great effort, I pushed it down. I turned to the others. I wasn't about to have this conversation with Tempest in front of them. "You have your assignments."

Grady stretched out his hand, making it clear he supported my leadership. "'When shall we three meet again in thunder, lightning, or in rain?'"

I automatically answered as I shook his hand, "'When the hurly-burly is done, when the battle's lost and won.'"

They left in their pairs, each one off to their assigned task.

"*MacBeth*?" Tempest said. "What was all that about?"

I sighed and ran my hand through my hair. I kept forgetting she couldn't be expected to know any of this, to understand why I was the one in charge. She didn't know what it meant to be a Qaniss. "It's what we say to each other when someone is leaving. Our farewell, I suppose you could call it."

With a start, I remembered asking my father what the term 'hurly-burly' meant. I could still hear him explaining that it was a Scots word for tumult...or tempest.

"You quote Shakespeare?"

Her question shook me out of my memory. I walked over to the stove where Harrison had been attempting to reheat the oatmeal he'd made yesterday. Out of all of us, he was best cook, though that wasn't saying much.

"He's the original founder," I said. "His words carry a lot of weight."

"So, what do you guys say when you're hungry? Because I could use a bite to eat."

Chapter Eleven

Tempest

"I'm curious," I said as I eyed a piece of dried fruit. "You said my mother was Susanna, daughter of William Shakespeare."

"I did." Bram leaned against the wall, watching me.

The intensity in his eyes was a little disconcerting, but I wasn't about to let him see that.

"Susanna Shakespeare married Dr. John Hall in 1607, right?"

He shook his head. "No. She married a blacksmith named Tobias Black in 1600 when she was seventeen."

I chewed the fruit slowly, taking time to turn over what he'd said. I knew that wasn't the case. I'd always loved Shakespeare. The way he turned a phrase. Literature had been the only kind of schoolwork at which I'd excelled.

"He had three children," I continued. "And Susanna married John Hall. They had a daughter, Elizabeth, a year later. She didn't have any kids. Shakespeare's family ended with her death."

"Maybe on this world," Bram said. "Any number of things could've factored into that. Perhaps Tobias Black was killed before he met Susanna or he was never born at all. That lead to her marrying John Hall."

I grimaced at the salty taste of the dried meat that made up the rest of my breakfast. "So you're saying my history's wrong?"

"Not wrong," he corrected. "Different. Parallel worlds, remember?"

I swallowed the last of the food and hoped there'd be better stuff than this later on. If I was going to spend the whole day training, I was going to need more to eat than what I'd had. At least there was plenty of water.

"Tell me about your Shakespeare, then," I said. "Did his son still die as a kid?"

Bram nodded. "And his daughter Judith had three children, none of whom made it to adulthood. The entire family was wiped out by demons in 1619 while they were trying to find out what happened to Susanna."

I felt a thrill go through me at my mother's name. Even though I knew it wasn't really her. It couldn't have been.

"What happened?" I drained the last of my drink, trying to look like I wasn't on edge, wanting to know.

He gave me a look that said he didn't believe my casual tone, but he didn't call me on it. "In 1602, when Susanna Black was nineteen, she and her husband were in London on a mission. She wasn't supposed to be there, of course, due to her pregnancy, but she was stubborn."

Well, at least I knew I came by that trait honestly. I shifted on the chair, uneasy at the thought. I hadn't accepted Susanna Shakespeare had been my mother.

Had I?

"They were ambushed. Tobias was left for dead and Susanna taken. No trace of her was ever found." He walked over to the door. "Ready?"

His quick change in topic didn't surprise me. I'd gotten the impression something about my past made him uncomfortable. Well, maybe not my past, but certainly my ancestry. Or, at least, the ancestry he claimed was mine. I wasn't about to ask him though. I didn't want him prying into my life, so I wasn't about to do it to him. Especially when there were more important things to worry about. Like this whole 'training to kill demons' thing.

"Let's go." I stood up.

I was wearing my jeans and tank-top, but I didn't bother with a jacket. I doubted I'd have to worry about being cold once we got started. As I followed him outside, I realized I wasn't actually cold right now. Sure, the wind was a bit brisk and I could smell a hint of snow in the air, but I wasn't shivering.

"We're going to warm up before we get started," Bram

said.

It was on the tip of my tongue to tell him I really didn't like the whole 'teacher' tone he had, but I didn't. He'd already said he wasn't a trainer. I could cut him a little slack. For now. If he started treating me like a child, we would have an issue.

"Stretch out." As he stretched, he talked. "You don't always have time to do this before a battle, but it's generally a good idea."

"I'm not a total idiot," I muttered as I stretched my back.

Bram gave me a sharp look that said he'd heard what I'd said. I didn't apologize.

"Qaniss don't need to stretch, just like we don't technically need to warm up," he continued. "Our bodies can take a lot of abuse before they give out." Something flashed across his eyes. "I've seen Qaniss lose a hand in battle, sear the stump to stop the bleeding ,and then return to the fight."

I straightened and shook out my arms. "What happened to you?"

He looked startled, as if my question had pulled him out of thoughts where I hadn't been present. "What?"

"Your side." I gestured towards his right side. "When I first saw you, you weren't wearing a shirt." Much to my annoyance, I could feel my face getting hot.

His eyes narrowed, and he studied me in silence for a

moment. Then his face went blank again. Shrugging, he pulled his shirt over his head.

I couldn't stop my eyes from widening. I'd thought I'd realized how bad the scars were the first time I'd seen them. Now I realized they were much worse.

What I'd seen yesterday had been a burn scar. I'd recognized the twisted, shiny look of the skin. It covered the entire top of his right shoulder and went down the right side of his chest. He turned slightly, showing me that it continued halfway down his back. It looked like someone had poured some kind of hot liquid or acid or something over his shoulder, and it had run down his body.

That wasn't the only scar he had either.

Starting at the top of his left shoulder and going across his chest down to his right hip were five jagged lines, almost as if someone had raked their nails across his skin. Or something, I thought. I didn't know anything about demon anatomy, but I was fairly confident at least one kind had claws.

"*Ardens Lingua*," he said, lightly touching the burn scar. "Literally means 'burning tongue' in Latin. Their saliva and blood are acidic."

"So that's because it, what, spit on you?"

A flicker of amusement went across his face and then disappeared. "I killed one, slit right through its belly. I hadn't realized my shirt had torn during the fight. My arm and hand were still protected, but its blood dripped through the opening at my shoulder and ran down my back and chest." He rubbed at his shoulder as if he could still feel the pain. "Would've been worse if it hadn't started raining. Washed away enough of the acid that I didn't end up with muscle damage."

"And those?" I gestured towards the five scars.

"An *excoriator* demon," he said.

"'Flayer'?" I translated from Latin. I suppressed a shiver. I could only imagine what those kinds of demons looked like.

"Claws on its hands and feet as well as razor-sharp teeth," Bram confirmed my mental image. He rolled his neck. "You speak Latin?"

I nodded. "I've always had a knack for languages."

"*Sprechen Sie Deutsch?*" he asked.

I gave him a tight smile. "Yes, I speak German. And French, Spanish, Greek, Russian and a bunch more. Are we going to talk about how many languages I can speak or are you going to teach me how to kill demons?"

"Not yet," he said. "First, we're going to run."

I gritted my teeth. I hated running. I was fast and in good shape, so that wasn't the reason. I hated it because it was boring. I wanted to do something more exciting. I knew it wouldn't do any good to argue though. Apparently, if I wanted to get to fighting, I had to run.

"Let's see if you can keep up. And I won't even use my wings."

I was going to offer a sharp retort, but then he took off and all I could do was stare. I'd never seen anyone move so fast. I started after him before I'd even realized I was going to do it. I'd always been quick, but even as my feet flew over the path, I could barely keep him in sight. I didn't know where we were going or if Bram had a particular destination in mind, but I followed him without thought, somehow knowing instinctively where to place my feet so they landed exactly where his had been. I wasn't gaining on him, but I had to be close to matching his pace since he wasn't pulling away.

After a while, my lungs began to burn. I wasn't sure if we'd been running for minutes or hours, but however long it had been, my body was starting to protest. My calves began to ache, but I refused to stop. I wasn't about to let him win. And I was sure that's what it was about. He was pushing me, trying to find my limits.

Gradually, he slowed and then stopped in the clearing surrounding the cabin. By the time I reached him, he was barely breathing any harder than he had been when we'd started. I glared at him as I jogged in place to keep from cramping up. So unfair.

"Not bad," he said. "Better than a normal person."

"Not as fast as you," I managed to gasp, hating myself for almost sounding weak.

"Give it time."

I scowled even though he didn't sound patronizing. After a minute or so, the stitch in my side faded and I was able to breathe more normally. "What do you have in mind now? Jumping jacks?"

Bram's lips twitched. "Not exactly."

He walked over to the edge of the woods and picked up two branches. They were long and fairly straight. I may not have grown up with a family, but I wasn't stupid. He was going to teach me to sword fight. With sticks.

"Seriously?" I raised an eyebrow as he held one of the sticks out to me.

"What sort of training do you have?" he asked. "What kind of fighting have you done?"

I held the end of the stick, testing the weight of it. At the small of my back was a real blade, albeit a small one.

"I wouldn't exactly call it training," I said. "More like necessity being the mother of invention."

His eyes flicked towards the side of my face where I'd been scarred eight years ago. I waited for the inevitable question, but it didn't come. No inquiry, no pity. It didn't surprise me though. People who had scars tended to understand how to react to others with them.

"I know how to use a knife," I admitted. I wasn't about to show him. My gut told me to trust him, but I was still wary.

"Good," he said, apparently pleased. "We'll check that out later, see what bad habits you need to lose."

I scowled at the assumption that I had bad habits to get rid of, but I didn't say anything. I had taught myself, after all. When it came to fighting, I wasn't too proud to take pointers. Humility was a small price to pay for survival.

"Right now, we're going to work on balance," Bram said. "How to move."

He gave me a once over and I flushed at the scrutiny.

"You're pretty graceful from what I've seen, so this should come easy for you."

I wasn't sure if he meant it as a compliment or an insult.

"I want you to mirror my movements." He took a stance with his feet shoulder distance apart, arms up, the far end of the stick balancing on his forearm.

I positioned my body to match his. Slowly, he began to move, raising one foot, turning at the waist. It almost looked like one of those intricate kinds of dances I'd seen in various cultures, the sort of dance that's supposed to tell a story of some kind. I followed his example, feeling foolish at first, but gradually settling into it.

I was surprised at how easy it was to lose myself in the movements. I usually considered myself a hyper-aware person, always cognizant of my surroundings. As I followed Bram, everything else sort of faded away, and I found myself matching him move for move. Even though I knew it was impossible, I almost felt like I knew how he would move next. And it wasn't like he was repeating the same sequence. More like I was tuned in to what he was going to do.

When we stopped, I was surprised to see that the sun was almost directly overhead. I was coated with a fine sheen of sweat, and my muscles felt like I'd been doing some sort of intense work out. I had a sinking feeling I was barely going to be able to walk tomorrow.

"Ready to show me what you've got?"

I raised an eyebrow and grinned, amused as his ears turned pink. "Do I get a knife or do you want me to use a stick?"

"Why don't you use the knife you already have?" he asked, regaining his composure quickly.

This time, it was my turn to be surprised.

"I felt it when I carried you into the cabin after Kassia knocked you out," he said. "Even if I hadn't, Lucan would've found it when he examined you."

"He did what?" My hand automatically went to the knife,

but not to show him how I fought. One of his buddies had been looking at me when I was passed out?

Something flickered across his eyes. "Just a basic exam to make sure you were okay. He's a healer. He didn't do anything inappropriate. He wouldn't have." There was a dark edge to his words that I didn't understand.

I still didn't relax, but I believed him that the guy he called Lucan hadn't messed with me. I was only wondering what else he'd seen. The scar on my face could've been from anything. The ones on my back, anyone with medical experience wouldn't mistake them for anything other than what they were. Again, I waited for the questions that didn't come.

"Are you going to use that thing, or think about it some more?" His voice was mild. "I'd like to see what we need to work on after lunch."

I pulled out my knife.

"How do you usually stand when you're ready to attack?"

I shrugged. "I don't have some sort of go-to stance or anything like that. I kinda roll with the punches. It's always self-defense."

"So what you're saying is, to see how well you fight, I have to attack you?" Bram raised an eyebrow.

I knew the idea of him coming at me for a fight should've frightened me. He was bigger and trained to kill things a lot scarier than me. Instead of fear, however, I got a thrill of anticipation, like there was some part of me that had been waiting for a fight, almost craving one. I straightened and put the knife away.

"What do you say we eat first?" I said. "I'm starving. Hitch-hiking from Ohio to Colorado doesn't include gourmet meals, and breakfast wasn't entirely appetizing."

He looked up at the sky, then at the road leading down the mountain. "The others should be back soon. We'll take a break when they get here."

He lunged towards me before I even realized he was coming.

Chapter Twelve

Bram

I'd never trained anyone before. I'd never even been trained in the traditional sense, as a pair. All Qaniss, until they were bonded, did individual training, but that had all been basic. Hand-to-hand combat, exercises designed to strengthen our bodies and our flexibility. We would study a bit on various weapons to see where our strengths were, but we never used weapons against someone until we bonded. True training didn't begin until then. For me, it had been with older Qaniss my father hired.

I didn't have the luxury of easing Tempest into things. She'd be getting thrown right in with eleven fairly seasoned fighters – even Tady had been training for several years – and I had absolutely no clue what I was doing. Still, I wasn't going to entrust the task to anyone else.

I hated the idea of hurting her during training, but I knew better than to hold back. Every Qaniss was taught from birth that we had a responsibility, and part of that meant we were never allowed to slack off. We trained in every form of weather, under every type of condition. Sick, injured, it didn't matter. If we were attacked, we knew the demons wouldn't take it easy on us because we happened to have a cold. We were Adonai's army. The last line of defense for mankind.

Tempest had never been through any of that and I could see it on her face. She didn't understand why I was pushing her, why I had no problem knocking her to the ground and then telling her to get up again without seeing if she was okay.

Or, at least, no problem she could see. Inside, I was fighting with myself. I hated seeing her hurt, seeing her wince in pain when I swept her legs out from underneath her and she crashed into the ground. I was only able to keep going by reminding myself if I didn't do this, she would never be able to survive against a demon. She'd be sore after sparring with me, but she'd be alive even if she made a mistake. That wouldn't be the case in a real fight.

After I knocked her down the second time, she started to get angry. That was good. I needed to see how she fought when her emotions ran high. Did it make her reckless, rushing into things without taking the time to analyze the situation? Or was she able to keep her cool, using her anger as fuel to give her strength and speed? Even without a bond, I could read the control on her face. She was struggling to keep herself in check, and managing to do it quite well.

I took a step towards her and she flipped the blade in her hand so she could use it multiple ways. That was good. Most people tried to jab with knives, and while that worked in close fighting, it didn't do any good if you wanted to keep your distance. You needed to be able to swing wide and the tip of a blade could only do so much damage.

Unfortunately for her, I had no problem grabbing her wrist and twisting until the knife fell onto the ground. She snatched it up and stomped a few feet away. She twisted her hair up behind her head, tucking it into place before settling into the defensive stance she'd been using.

"Again," she snapped.

I came at her and disarmed her in only a few seconds. Her eyes flashed as she let out a stream of curses. When she turned back towards me, I could see how upset she was. Still, I didn't call off.

Instead, I motioned for her to come at me.

When her knife fell for the third time, she didn't even bother to pick it back up. She marched past me towards Emilia and Harrison, her face bright red. I wanted to tell her not to be embarrassed, that I'd been fighting for years, and there was no way she could've beaten me. Somehow, though, I sensed telling her that would only make her more angry.

I sighed. "All right, Adonai," I said quietly. "I'd love to know what Your plan is here because I don't see how she's going to be any good to us in the near future."

I wasn't surprised when I didn't get an answer. When it

came to sharing His plans, I'd never been on the top of Adonai's list.

Chapter Thirteen

Tempest

Every part of me hurt. My head, my muscles, my joints...

Bram had kicked my butt three times before Emilia and Harrison came back, disarming me each time, and he hadn't even pulled out his wings. I'd hesitated to pull the knife the first time, worrying I'd hurt him, but it hadn't taken me long to see there was no way I'd get close enough to hurt him. I'd never seen anyone move like him, not in real life. I'd gotten the sense he was holding back, which made it worse.

I was outside again, alone this time. Things had been tense when I'd tried to help in the little kitchen, but I'd been hoping it was because the space was small, or because Harrison and Emilia were always in their own little world. But then some of the others had come back, and it had been clear to me I was the reason things were weird.

I took a deep breath of the cool autumn air. It was going to snow soon. I ran my hands through my hair. I'd lost all track of time while traveling. What was I doing here? Following some hunch that took me across the country to a group of demon hunters who I was supposedly a part of? Oh, and to top it all off, I was the grand-daughter of the good old Bard.

"Needed some space, *a nighean*?"

I turned to see the little red-head coming towards me. Tady, I remembered. Tady Wells. I was surprised to see her alone. I never really saw any of them alone. Well, anyone but Bram. The rest of them always seemed to have another close by. Always the same one too. For Tady, it was the green-eyed boy I'd seen hovering around her. I glanced at the cabin. Sure enough, there he was. Bair. He was leaning in the doorway, watching Tady as she walked towards me.

"It gets a wee bit crowded in there," she said. "And comin' from me, that says a lot. I like havin' lots of people around. I'd always wished I had brothers and sisters." Her expression clouded. "Now, I'm almost glad I didn't."

"I'm sorry." The words came out automatically, but I found I meant them. Of all of them, Tady was the most approachable. I got the impression she was as tough as the others, but there was still something about her that made her seem more vulnerable. I started to ask the question that had been bouncing around in my head for a while, but then I hesitated. I wasn't sure I could bring myself to say it to her.

"Ask," she said softly. "I kin see the question on yer face."

"What happened?" I kept my voice low, unsure how sharp their hearing was. I'd gotten the impression no one wanted to talk about it.

"To keep it brief." Her face was tight. "Our world is gone.

End of days came. Judgement. Reward and punishment. All the things in Revelations. We are all that's left."

"Revelations? You mean like the Bible? Armageddon? The Apocalypse?"

"The signs had been there," Tady said. She turned so she was looking down the mountain. Her accent thickened as she spoke. "But none was certain. We dinna *fash* ourselves about it. I suppose that was why everythin' was always so vague, so we'd be sure to rely on faith. None of us thought of what it would mean to anyone who weren't there when it happened."

She fell silent long enough that I wasn't sure she was going to continue, but before I could say anything, she started talking again.

"The *deamhan* became more bold on our world, requirin' a greater number of Qaniss to stay 'n fight there until, finally, only a handful were bein' sent out to other worlds. I dinna ken how much the Council knew about what was coming, but they dinna tell us much." She looked down at her hands.

She had the same small scars on her fingers and palm that Bram did. I wondered if my hands would look the same after a while. If I stayed with them. I hadn't made my mind up yet. Or that's what I told myself.

"We'd thought we'd be there at the end, with our families. Either that or already dead, waitin' for those who were livin' to join us. We never thought we'd be asked to stay behind." She glanced towards the cabin to where Bair was still standing. "Bair and I at least never thought it." She gave me a smile that didn't reach her eyes. "I'm not sure what the others thought, or if they'd even considered it until..." Her voice trailed off.

I felt bad now, having brought up something so painful. I could only imagine what it would be like to suddenly lose everyone and everything in one fell swoop. I tried changing the subject. "At least you have Bair. How long have the two of you been dating?"

Tady's face went pink. "We're not – I mean, we..."

"Oh, I'm sorry." I backpedaled. "I assumed the two of you..." I looked over at him. "You're always together."

"We are bonded, so..." Tady's eyes widened when I gave her a blank look. "Bram dinna tell ye about bonds?"

"No." I shook my head. "He told me what you guys were. What I'm supposed to be. He sort of explained the whole parallel world thing." I frowned. "And Shakespeare was my grandfather."

"Aye, that one's a bit odd, even for us."

The fact that Tady admitted it wasn't normal for them made me actually feel better about the idea. I wasn't going there though. I wanted to hear more about this bonding. From how it sounded, it might explain the whole weird paired off thing. Five couples and one guy were the only survivors from an entire planet? The odds weren't exactly likely.

"So what's this bonded thing?"

Tady suddenly looked nervous. "I'm not sure if I'm the best one to explain it to ye."

I turned as if I was planning on walking away. "I'll go ask Bram them."

"Wait." Tady sighed. "I dinna think he's in the best mood right now."

I turned back towards her. I didn't doubt he was annoyed at me at the moment.

"The power Adonai gave the Qaniss was too great for a single person to handle alone." Tady sounded like she was reciting from some lecture she'd heard a million times. "By the age of twelve, virtually every Qaniss is bonded with another. We share the power between us. We kin sense each other's emotions, and if we need to, communicate telepathically."

"You can read each other's minds?"

"Not exactly," Tady said. "More like talk with our minds. We canna dig in to somethin' our bonded doesna want us to see or anythin' like that. Not that we hide anythin' from each other. Why would we?"

I could answer that question. There were a million things I wouldn't want to share with anyone.

"I suppose it would be harder," Tady continued, a thoughtful expression on her face. "If we dinna bond so young. Most of find our bonded around ten or so, but twelve's always the cut-off. Once we claim our bonded, we receive our tattoos and the bondin' takes place."

I put my hand over my wrist before I'd realized I was going to do it. "What do the tattoos have to do with it?"

"They're imbued with Adonai's power and done at the same time, part of the ritual sharing the power between them. That's when we get our wings, too."

I rubbed my wrist, trying not to think of what it had felt like to touch Bram's tattoo. "I thought you said you and Bair weren't dating? Is it because it's something more than that? Like you're engaged?"

Tady flushed again and I saw her shoot a look towards where Bair was standing. "No. About half of all bonded pairs get married to each other, but the rest either don't marry or they fall in love with someone else."

I was intrigued despite myself. "How does it work? This bonding thing? Is it like some sort of arranged marriage, like your parents pick your partner?"

Tady shook her head. "It's hard to explain. You see them, and it's there, this connection. It's like a tug inside ye, pulling ye both together. And when yer bonded, it's like you've only been a half a person 'til that point."

"So, what happened to Bram's bonded?" I hoped my voice sounded more casual to her than it did to me. I wasn't sure why it mattered though. I wasn't interested in Bram. Not that way. Not any way. "Was he – or she – left behind when you guys came here?"

Tady shook her head, looking even more uncomfortable than before. "Almost all bonded die within days of each other. They canna handle the power on their own." She took a step closer to me and lowered her voice. "Bram's the only exception. When he was twelve, he still hadna bonded with anyone. There's never more than a couple years age difference between pairs, so everyone knew it wasna like his bonded hadna been born yet. Every Qaniss around his age wanted to be bonded with him, and with his father leadin' the Council, it was quite a big deal he hadn't bonded yet."

"I thought you said the Qaniss received their tattoos as a bonded pair." I focused on my question rather than the surprise at hearing Bram's father was the leader – had been the leader, I reminded myself – of this group of demon hunters.

"They do," Tady said. "Except Bram. He demanded to receive the tattoo even though everyone ken it would kill him. It twas too much power for one person to handle alone. But he insisted. It was either try it and die, or live as one of the few

Qaniss who dinna bond. They became historians and teachers mostly. They canna ever fight."

Even though I'd only known Bram a short time, I knew neither of those options would've worked for him. It didn't surprise me he'd taken the risk.

"I was there," she said. "I was only nine, but I remember it. Bair and I had just found each other and we were goin' to be bonded a few days later. We were standin' together, watchin' Bram walk up to the platform alone, his chin up, eyes straight ahead."

I could almost picture it, a much younger Bram, with those same slate gray eyes, determined and unafraid.

"Some Qaniss *skelloch*, scream, ye ken, when they receive their tattoos. The power, it's overwhelming even with two. Bram dinna make a sound. He gritted his teeth and his muscles were all clenched, but not a single sound. Everyone kept waitin' for him to collapse, for his heart to give out, but he stayed awake through all of it. Even when his wings came, and I kin tell ye, that's a pain like nothin' ye'd ever felt before." The admiration in her voice was clear. "Bram is the only Qaniss to ever survive receivin' Adonai's power alone."

I looked back at the cabin again. It seemed there was more to my trainer than I'd first realized.

Chapter Fourteen

Bram

I watched the pair through the window, catching enough of what Tady was saying to know she was telling Tempest about bonding. I should've been the one to tell her. Not only because I was supposed to be the leader now, but because of what I knew. I'd felt it the moment I'd first seen her, the sharp tug inside me that I'd been told about, but had never experienced. It shouldn't have been possible, not at my age, but there was no mistaking it. She was supposed to be bonded with me. She was mine.

I turned away from the window, and walked over to the door. I needed some space. Bair glanced at me as I walked by, but I didn't say anything to him. I liked the kid well enough, but I didn't want to talk to anyone right now. Even though every fiber in my being begged me to go to Tempest, to talk to her, bond with her, I went the other way. I couldn't do it. Not yet. Not until I understood.

"All right, Adonai," I muttered as I disappeared into the thick wood next to the cabin. "I need you to tell me what to do because I have absolutely no clue."

The silence was expected. I'd been trying to pray a lot since Vitor had come to us, but I hadn't really gotten anything in the way of responses. As the only Qaniss to survive holding the power alone, most people assumed I must have had something in the way of a special connection to Adonai. Even my father had thought it. I'd never told anyone that I sometimes felt the exact opposite, that perhaps Adonai thought because I had more power than the others, He didn't need to talk to me quite as much.

I was alone in more ways than one.

As I always did when I started getting maudlin, my hand rubbed the claw scars running across my chest. I hadn't bothered to put my shirt back on after training and I could feel the subtle difference in the scar tissue.

I sometimes wondered if the demon would've caught me off guard if I'd been bonded. If I'd had someone to watch my back. It might not have made a difference. After all, Grady had been bonded when he'd lost his eye. And the others were scarred as well. I hadn't heard all their stories of how they'd gotten each one, but I had no doubt it involved two of them.

I'd been alone when the *excoriator* had attacked. Thirteen and still not fully in control of my power, I'd been out by the river that had run behind my house, trying to practice, when I'd heard a noise.

I closed my eyes. I could still recall every detail.

****

My hands were shaking and I clenched them into fists. It would pass, I knew. It happened less frequently than it had when I'd first taken the tattoo. I'd barely been able to stand the first few days after, my entire body trembling.

I still couldn't believe I'd been able to walk off the platform on my own, my new wings dragging behind me, my back and shoulders screaming. My father had said it was because Adonai had blessed me, additional proof of His favor, he'd claimed. The first evidence, of course, had been my initial survival. In the recorded history of the Qaniss, only a handful of Qaniss had ever tried to absorb the power alone, and every one of them had died. All Qaniss were taught the stories, as much to discourage the power-hungry as to explain why we all bonded.

Except I hadn't. It wasn't completely rare, but it wasn't exactly common either. Maybe half a dozen every generation or so didn't find their bonded. No one knew why it happened.

Some speculated Adonai had chosen those people to serve in a capacity other than fighting, and this was the way to ensure it. Others believed it was a simpler, biological explanation. The one we'd been intended for had died. A miscarriage or died at birth or in childhood. A pregnant Qaniss killed in battle – again, rare since, as soon as a Qaniss learned she was with child, she was pulled from the battlefield. We weren't a populous people. Pregnancy wasn't easy for our kind and an early death was more common than a late one.

My own mother had died giving birth to me.

I pushed the thought from my head. The power was harder to control when I was emotional. I'd spent the last year learning how to keep down my emotions. I supposed that was one of the reasons why the bonding was so important. Bonded could share emotions, support each other. I had to deal with everything on my own.

I closed my eyes and tried to focus the energy inside me. I'd spent a year learning to control myself. Now I had to learn how to let out what I needed, when I needed it. I was only supposed to practice with Mr. Waite, the tutor my father had hired. Until I had my powers under control, I wouldn't be going back to school.

I didn't really mind. I'd gotten my fill of being stared at within the first month. Now, I tried to avoid people as much as possible. If I'd accepted the life of the non-bonded, the attention and pity would have faded after a few weeks. Me, I was something new. Unique. People were going to stare at me for the rest of my life unless someone else did what I'd done. Considering I was the first since the beginning of time, the chances of it happening again seemed sort of doubtful to say the least.

I gritted my teeth as I crouched down. The first thing a Qaniss learned to use as a channel for their power was the earth itself. Pushing power into the ground ran less of a risk of accidentally harming someone than putting it into a weapon of some kind. Unless, of course, the person doing it was me. I'd thrown Mr. Waite three feet in the air, and then back another four feet. He hadn't been badly hurt, just bruised and the wind knocked out of him, but that had ended our lessons for the day. Now I had the weekend off.

I put my palms on the ground and tried to do what Mr. Waite had said. Picture the power coming up from the well inside me where I stored it. Envision it flowing down my arms and into my hands, my fingers. Then imagine I was pushing it into the ground.

I was concentrating so hard on what I was doing, I didn't realize I wasn't alone until it was too late. I heard the rush of air, smelled the stench of hell, and I spun around. It was stupid, I knew. I had no weapons, no way to fight back unless I could manage a burst of power like I had yesterday, and that had been an accident. No Qaniss had ever use straight power on a demon. It didn't work. There wasn't enough of it.

I barely had time to register the teeth and claws before it was on me. Burning pain ran across my chest and I felt the heat of blood on my skin. Then the calm of battle was on me, the kind of crystal clarity I'd only heard about.

Without thinking about what I was doing, I grabbed the demon around its throat. The scaly skin was hot against my palms, painfully so, but I didn't let go. It was an excoriator *demon, the kind that had spawned myths of dragons on many worlds. Its teeth were broken and jagged, and I knew if I didn't hold it off, one bite could end me. It raised its hands, the claws on the ends of its fingers as cruel as its teeth, and I knew I was dead.*

Suddenly, a burst of power went through me. I felt it race up my arms and into my hands. Without thinking, I pushed.

There was a moment of surprise on the demon's face, and then it exploded. Not the face. Or, at least, not only the face. The entire thing exploded in a shower of blood and gore...

****

I'd been too shocked to scream after it had happened, even though I'd felt the sound growing in my chest. By the time I'd regained enough breath to manage it, I'd had myself under control again. I'd stood up and headed back into the house. I'd managed to avoid my father until I'd washed myself and changed into a clean pair of pants. I hadn't bothered with a new shirt. I'd known stitches were going to be needed for the cuts its claws had made. I'd told my father I'd been attacked by an *excoriator,* but I'd made it sound like I'd managed a lucky swing with a sword, injuring the demon enough that it had fled. Even that had been quite the story.

I'd never told anyone what had really happened. As far as I knew, no Qaniss had ever done what I'd done, and I hadn't wanted to give them anything new to make me feel like I was freak. I'd never tried to do it again. I didn't know if I could and I hadn't wanted to risk it. Not to mention how badly it had scared me. The feel of so much power, coursing up my arms...

I was so absorbed in my thoughts that it wasn't until I heard a yell that I realized something was happening at the cabin.

I took off running before my brain had fully processed the situation, my wings immediately full and flexing. As I ran, however, my mind caught up, and by the time I reached the clearing, the battle cold had come over me and I saw everything with pristine sharpness.

The Qaniss were spread out, each pair fighting two demons at once. The stench was overwhelming.

Annabella and Grady were a blur of blades and feathers as they hacked at a pair of *cropian llyngyr*, a huge, worm-like demon with fangs and coils that could squeeze a person to death in minutes.

Leigh and Lucan were nearby ,but I couldn't see what weapons they had. Between the *ardens lingua* and *excoriator* they were fighting and their wings, I could only see glimpses of them.

Another *excoriator* was attacking Emilia and Harrison alongside a *spinis*. The foot-long spines down its back were wicked-looking, as were the ones on its knuckles. As I watched, one of Emilia's pale blue wings whipped out and knocked the legs out from under the creature.

Tady and Bair were taking on a pair of *beach cliseadh*, the large 'stinging bee' that looked like a cross between a wasp and a scorpion. Tady's face was red and I could see Bair working twice as hard to put himself between his bonded and danger. All four were in the air, Tady and Bair swooping and diving as their blades flashed.

An *ardens lingua* and another *spinis* were being beaten back by Kassia and Fynn as they stood side-by-side, swords in hand. With Fynn being left-handed, they made a formidable pair. I'd never seen anyone fight that way.

I grabbed the ax from where'd I'd last left it and took a step forward to join in the battle. Something inside me jerked sharply and I froze. Five pairs.

Where was Tempest?

For a split second, panic nearly overwhelmed me. I'd just

found her. I couldn't lose her.

Then I heard it. The sounds of another scuffle, apart from the others. I didn't hesitate as I turned and ran towards it. For the first time in my life, my mind wasn't on what demon I would find, but on the person fighting. I had to get to her. We needed her. *I* needed her.

When I saw the demon, my blood ran cold. Of all the demons we fought, the *vihane surma* were the ones I feared the most. It didn't look as dangerous as the others, being almost human in appearance, but its skin secreted poison. One touch against bare skin and a person would die a horrible, painful death. I'd seen it happen.

And Tempest was fighting it with her little switchblade.

I could see the creature looking for an opening, any chance to grab onto Tempest's bare arms. Her jacket was on the ground, probably because it was easier to move without it, but she didn't know how much more danger she was in now because she'd taken it off.

All this went through my head in the few seconds it took me to run towards her, tucking my wings close. I was two steps away, ready to swing my ax, and her eyes flicked towards me. The smallest of movements, involuntary most likely, but it was enough of a warning to the demon that it was able to move out of the way of my swing.

It spun, and Tempest lunged at it, eyes flashing, a determined expression on her face. I saw the demon's hand reaching for her and didn't even think. I threw myself between them, grabbing her as I went. We tumbled to the ground and Tempest let out a squeak of half-surprise, half-annoyance. As soon as we hit, I rolled, bringing up my ax as I went. I shoved power into the weapon, the air going out of my lungs at the intensity of the energy coursing through me. It was stronger than anything I'd ever felt before and, for a moment, I wondered if the ax would be able to take it. I'd exploded more than one weapon during training as a child.

The ax vibrated in my hand as the iron sliced through the demon's hand. I felt its shock as I allowed my momentum to give the ax enough force to slice clean through the demon's neck. Its head bounced onto the ground. I kept the ax in hand as I turned, immediately looking for any other threat. The only thing I saw was Tempest, glaring at me as she got to her feet.

I started to take a step forward when pain shot through me. My knees buckled and, as I went down, the world began to gray out. I was dimly aware of Tempest calling my name and then everything went dark, leaving me only with pain and the black.

Chapter Fifteen

Tempest

My hands were trembling and I didn't know why. It could've been shock from fighting the demon. At least, I assumed that's what it had been. It had looked human, sort of. Hairless, with sickly pale white skin. Its eyes had been red and there'd been no mouth. Not like its mouth had been sewn up or anything like that. No mouth at all. And there were certain other things missing too. Let's say I couldn't tell if the demon had been male or female and it hadn't been wearing clothes.

It had to be from fighting the demon. From seeing Bram cut off its head.

Bram.

"Tempest!"

Tady shook me and my attention snapped back to her. Her face was streaked with a nasty black ichor I guessed was demon blood.

"We have to get him inside." Her voice was hard, so different from her usual tone that it broke through to me.

I swallowed hard and nodded. I forced myself to look down as Tady and I got our hands under Bram's arms. My stomach twisted as I tried to lift his limp body. Everything had happened so fast.

One minute, I'd been standing there, talking to Tady, then she'd started running towards Bair. I'd tried to go too, but that...thing had gotten in the way. Then Bram had been there. Knocked me to the ground and killed it. I hadn't seen him get hurt, but he'd just collapsed.

"What happened?!" Lucan shouted.

I looked up to see the others running towards us. Fynn and Bair quickly took Bram from us and started running towards the cabin, Bram's feet dragging behind them. Lucan grabbed my arm, his grip almost painful. He pulled me after him, but I didn't need the incentive to run. My heart was pounding and I knew something was wrong. Wrong with Bram, and that scared me more than I thought it should.

Fynn and Bair had Bram on the bed in the back by the time Lucan and I reached the bedroom doorway. The other Qaniss were in the main room, all of them sporting various signs of having been in a fight. No one seemed to be worried about any of their own injuries though.

"What happened?" Lucan repeated his question as he knelt bent over Bram.

"I don't know." I shook my head, hating that I couldn't answer his question. "I was fighting this demon-thing and Bram jumped in. He cut off its hand and then its head with an ax. I thought he was fine, but he collapsed."

"Hand?" Lucan froze. He didn't look up at me and his voice was pitched low, like he didn't want anyone else to hear his question.

"Yeah," I said.

"Tempest, what did it look like?"

"The demon? Kind of like a person, I guess..."

I didn't bother with any other description because I knew immediately that Lucan knew what it had been. His entire body went stiff, and he let out a string of words I didn't know. The tone told me they weren't anything good.

"Lucan?" Annabella spoke up from the doorway.

"*Vihane surma.*"

I had no idea what that meant, but the way the color drained from Annabella's face made my heart thump painfully against my chest. Of all the others, she was the only one I thought of as being as tough as Bram.

"*A Dhia, thoir cobhair,*" Tady whispered.

After a moment without further explanation, I finally asked, "Will someone tell me what's going on?"

Lucan pointed to four dark spots on Bram's shoulder. Dark spots that hadn't been there before. He rolled Bram over to reveal a fifth spot right above his shoulder-blade.

"It grabbed his shoulder." He glanced up at me now, his expression haggard. "It's poison, Tempest. The *vihane surma*'s skin secretes it."

In my mind's eye, I saw the demon reaching for me. Saw Bram throwing himself at me. Between me and the demon's deadly touch.

"So give him the antidote," I said.

"There's nothing I can do." Lucan stood. "No cure. The poison works its way through the skin and into the muscles, destroying everything." His face tightened. "The healthier the person, the longer it takes. The more pain they're in. He'll regain consciousness soon and wish he hadn't."

"Cut it out."

He blinked, startled by my statement almost as much as I was. Where had that come from? I knew a bit about first aid, but I wasn't even close to being a medical professional. I didn't even know if Qaniss anatomy was the same as a regular human. Still, something deep in my gut told me to say it again and explain.

"Cut out the poisoned pieces. Cauterize the wounds. It'll stop the poison from spreading."

Lucan stared at me for a moment, then called over his shoulder, "Leigh, bring me my medical bag."

"You're not serious?!" Annabella snapped. "You can't do that."

Lucan gave her a steady look, but didn't say a word as

Leigh handed him a bag.

"It's her decision to make," Leigh said to her sister.

I didn't ask what Leigh was talking about. I already knew. Of course I did. From the moment Tady had told me about pairs bonding, I'd known. I didn't understand it, but that didn't change anything.

I sat on the edge of the bed and looked at Lucan. My hands weren't shaking anymore. "Do it."

"I can't promise this'll work," Lucan said. "And I don't know how deep the poison's gone."

"Then you'd better hurry," I said.

"I'm going to need someone to hold him down," he said. "Can you do it?"

I nodded. It didn't matter how much bigger Bram was than me. He'd gotten hurt protecting me. I owed him my life. I climbed onto the bed, straddling his waist and putting one hand on his uninjured shoulder, the other on his left wrist. I was glad it wasn't the right wrist. I didn't want to know what would happen if I touched his tattoo again.

"She won't be able to hold him alone," Annabella said, shooting me a dark look.

Lucan glanced at me and then looked at her. "Everyone else out."

I waited for her to argue again, but she didn't. That alone

told me how serious Bram's condition was. I didn't want to watch what Lucan was going to do, but I refused to let myself look away. I wasn't yet sure if I wanted to become a part of them, but I knew if I did, I had to show I was strong. My stomach lurched and I tightened my grip, mentally preparing myself.

Bram didn't move with the first cut, but as Lucan continued, digging deep into the flesh, Bram's eyes opened. For a moment, they were wide, wild with pain and confusion, and then they met mine. I felt an almost audible click and I was suddenly acutely aware of every inch of Bram's body. It was like nothing I'd ever felt before. It was more than the sensation of his muscles tensing under my fingers, his body struggling against the pain. I could feel the knife cutting through skin and flesh. Feel his heart beating wildly. His teeth grinding together as he writhed in pain.

My own body was tense, heart pounding against my ribs. The smell of blood was so thick I could taste it, that copper tang I knew so well. His entire body jerked, and then I smelled burning flesh, heard the sizzle.

"Look at me," I muttered, willing him to do just that. I didn't know why, only that I knew it was what he needed. His eyes locked with mine again.

I felt more than saw him raising his hand, and I

automatically moved to push the hand down.

A surge of energy went through me, like nothing I'd ever felt before.

As a child, I'd always been fascinated by storms. I'd always supposed it had been a combination of my name and the fact that I'd been told I'd been born during a freak storm. I'd loved hearing the thunder, feeling the rush of the wind. But, most of all, I'd loved lightning. The power and beauty of it. The danger. When all of the other children had cowered in their beds in fear, I'd been at the window, watching. Over the years, I'd wondered what it would feel like to be close to a lightning strike, to feel the strike itself. Not because I'd had a death wish, but simply because I thought the power from such a release of electricity must've been incredible.

This was what it must've felt like, I thought as the little hairs all across my body stood on end. I could feel the static electricity crackle around me, the air thick with the smell of ozone.

I tried to pull my hand away as my brain finally registered the pain racing across my nerves, but it wouldn't budge. I'd felt worse, but this wasn't exactly pleasant. I was dimly aware of noise, but it didn't seem real. The only real things were myself and Bram, and the power flowing between us.

Suddenly, he jerked away, breaking the connection, and I

fell backwards, landing at the end of the bed.

"What," I managed to gasp. "What happened?"

Lucan stared at me with wide eyes, the expression on his face scaring me more than what had happened. The door slammed open and the others were all there, weapons drawn.

"Put them down."

Their eyes turned towards Bram at his command and I let my gaze follow. He was sitting up, his chest and back covered with blood. The places were the demon's fingers had been were burnt, skin and muscle blackened and raw, but his voice was strong. His wings were out, the tips flicking at the air. He was still pale, but not as much as he had been. He hissed as he gingerly moved his arm, glaring at Lucan when the other man tried to stop him.

"I'm okay," Bram insisted. "The poison, it's gone."

"That shouldn't have worked," Annabella said. She flushed when her sister gave her a sharp look. "I'm glad it did, but it shouldn't have. No one's ever survived the touch of a *vihane surma.*"

"Well, I suppose there's a first time for everything," Bram said, his tone almost absent as his fingers moved over the wounds, not touching, but rather tracing the air above the skin.

"How did you get your power to heal him?" Annabella demanded. "I knew you had skill as a healer, Lucan, but I didn't know you could release that much into a person."

"I can't," Lucan said. He looked at me and I shifted uncomfortably. "What happened?"

I shook my head. "I don't know." I glanced at Bram but he wasn't looking at me. "I think I accidentally touched his tattoo."

"That only causes a minor flare of power from a bonded pair," Emilia spoke up.

"These aren't exactly normal circumstances." It was the first time I'd heard Harrison speak. His voice was soft, but clear. "There's never been anything like either of them before."

"Harrison's right," Bram said. "The rules have bent for me before."

I felt safe in assuming he was referring to his status as the only Qaniss who'd ever survived receiving his power alone. What, I wondered, did that mean for me? If what had happened was any indication, we had some serious power between the two of us, and it wasn't anything normal.

"I could feel it," Bram continued. "The energy going through me, cleaning out the poison that had already begun to seep into my bones. What Lucan did might've worked if it had been done immediately, but it was too late for me. I would've died without Tempest being here."

He looked up at me now, but I couldn't read a thing on his

face. I could feel the others watching me too, and I didn't need any supernatural powers to feel the confusion, wariness and even some resentment coming from them.

"Thank you." He tipped his head in a bit of a bow.

"Guess we're even now." I crossed my arms. I could feel my defenses slamming into place. "But you wouldn't have needed me to save you if you hadn't been dumb enough to push me out of the way in the first place."

His eyes darkened and I heard the others expressing varying degrees of surprise and disgust at my comment. I ignored them. This was between Bram and me.

"I think I'm good here, Lucan," Bram said without taking his eyes off of me. "I think Tempest and I need to have a bit of a talk."

Chapter Sixteen

Bram

My hands were shaking from what had happened – the power surge, not the near-death experience. I'd had those before. What I'd never experienced before was the kind of energy being shoved into me through my tattoo. It had been raw, wild, and I'd known, without consciously thinking of it, that this had been the kind of power Adonai had used to speak creation into being. My wings were still twitching.

Most Qaniss power was the same, a destructive, but muted energy. Those with an aptitude for healing, such as Lucan, always had a touch of the other sort of power mixed in. It wasn't something they could consciously control though. More like they radiated it so it assisted in the healing. Sped it up. What Tempest had done, however, wasn't anything I'd ever seen or heard before. A sharp, twisted pain went through me as I felt my father's loss more deeply than before. He would've known what to do.

All of this raced through my mind in a matter of seconds, and by the time I'd pushed it aside, the others were gone and Tempest and I were alone. She'd stood up and I could almost feel the shields she'd put into place.

What had happened had affected her in more ways than

one. The power frightened her, and it was good it did. Qaniss who weren't afraid of Adonai's power at first never learned a healthy respect for it, and without that...well, while it hadn't been commonplace, there had been Qaniss who'd needed to be put down.

It wasn't only fear of the power I felt from her, however. We weren't bonded, but I could feel her nonetheless, even more so now that her power was still flowing through my body. She was scared, and angry. I was pretty sure most of the latter was directed at me.

"Is this where you give me some smart remark about how that thing would've killed me if you hadn't stopped it?"

Her tone was sharp, and my temper automatically rose against it. I pushed it back. I'd had years of practice tamping it down and it was easy enough to keep my voice calm.

"Not a smart remark, but rather the truth. You weren't ready to fight any demon, much less a *vihane surma*. You didn't know that a single touch could kill you."

"I was doing fine on my own." Her chin was up, jaw clenched.

"Your switchblade wasn't going to work on a demon. Not that demon, not even if you knew how to give your weapon power." I tried not to sound condescending, but the way Tempest was stiffening, I knew she'd taken it the wrong way.

"Well, I guess I would've figured it out on my own."

"And you would've been dead!" I snapped, the end of my wing flicking against the wall. What was it about this girl that riled me up so much? I pushed the question aside. I didn't want to know the answer.

"Guess so." She shrugged.

It was the gesture that did it. The casual way she accepted that she'd be dead.

"What good would that have done?" I stood up, fighting the wave of dizziness that hit me. I flapped my wings to steady me. "We need you alive."

She rolled her eyes and made a derisive sound. "You said yourself I don't know what I'm doing. I'm not a Qaniss. I'm a foster kid from Ohio who happens to have a tattoo."

"After what you did, you still believe that?"

She ignored my question. "You guys don't need me."

"Yes," I said. "I do."

I saw the startled look at my word choice, breaking her mask for a moment before she recovered.

"Yeah, well, too bad." She walked over to the window. "I'm not staying. You saved my life, I saved yours. We're even."

"No we're not. I saved your life twice." I knew the words were a mistake as soon as I said them, but I'd needed to say something. I couldn't just let her go. She was one of us. More than that, she was mine. I'd spent the last seven years more alone than I'd thought possible. I wasn't about to go back to that without a fight.

"No one asked you to save me." Her voice was hard. "I'm not some damsel in distress who needs rescuing."

I was about to point out that she had, actually, needed to be rescued both times, but the door opened, stopping me. When I caught a glimpse of the fire in Tempest's eyes and felt a wave of hostility, I had to admit it was probably for the best I hadn't said anything.

"Bram, sorry, but we kind of have a time sensitive situation here." Grady sounded mildly apologetic, which was better than how Annabella would've been if she'd interrupted. Probably why he'd been the one to come in.

"What is it?" I was glad my hands were steady again. I could still feel the extra power in me, twitching muscles and nerves, but I had it under control.

"Kassia and Fynn managed to capture the *spinis* they were fighting."

I blinked. "Why would they do that?"

Grady's expression was grim. "Because we suddenly realized we're fighting blind here, *mon ami*."

I didn't need him to explain now. I got it, but I had to say it out loud for Tempest's benefit. She was pissed at me right now and said she wasn't staying, but I wasn't going to accept that, so she needed to understand.

"Without the Council back home to give us our missions, we need to find out what the demons are up to another way."

Grady's single eye, bright and intelligent, glanced at Tempest and then back at me. He knew why I'd said it, but he wasn't going to call attention to it. Smart man. Then again, being bonded to Annabella must've made him quite an expert at handling women who were a bit...tempestuous was the word that automatically came to mind.

"We figured we could question it before we killed it," he said. "It's out in the woodshed."

I nodded. "Who's guarding it?"

"Annabella helped Kassia bind it," Grady explained. "Plus it's wounded, so it's not putting up much of a fight."

I thought about putting on a shirt, but decided against it. I already had a bit of a reputation among the demons since I fought alone, but if the *spinis* saw I'd survived *vihane surma* poison, maybe it'd give us the information relatively quickly. I had energy at the moment, but I didn't know how long it would last. I didn't even want to think about what would happen if I collapsed in the middle of interrogating a demon, even with back-up there.

"What are you going to do?"

I'd almost forgotten about Tempest. Almost. I doubted she'd ever really be gone from my head. She was like a buzzing in the back of my head, almost like white noise, but not annoying, just...there.

"We're going to interrogate our prisoner," I said.

"You mean you're going to torture him, then kill him." Her voice was flat.

I jerked my chin towards the door and Grady nodded, then headed out. I turned back towards Tempest to find her facing me, arms still crossed.

"It's a demon. Not a him. Not a her." She needed to understand this if she was going to be one of us. "Do you know how demons came to be?"

She made a face. "Something about Satan and apples?"

I wanted to smile, but I knew she'd take it the wrong way so I kept my expression serious. "Not quite. Lucifer was an angel, one of Adonai's most beautiful creations, but he became proud and thought he should rule heaven. One third of the angels agreed, and they were all banished, kicked out of heaven. They became demons and their true forms were twisted as they embraced the darkness. Demons are fallen angels, no gender. They aren't human."

"Kind of like animals?" She raised an eyebrow. "Would

you be okay torturing them too?"

I shook my head. "No. Animals are innocent."

"I don't–"

"You don't have to be there," I interrupted. I wanted her there, needed her actually, but I wasn't going to push. It'd be worse if she wasn't ready.

"No." She shook her head, a stubborn look coming over her face. "I'm coming. I have to see for myself."

I gave her a terse nod. I wasn't entirely sure I liked the idea of her seeing something that might end up being fairly gruesome, and I knew I didn't want her to see me in a negative light, but all of that had to be secondary to our calling. Even though we hadn't bonded, if she wasn't with me, I'd be wondering where she was, what she was thinking, and I couldn't afford to be distracted at the moment.

The two of us walked out of the room and found the others waiting, all still streaked with blood and dirt. I could tell they'd all been anxious. There were so few of us that none of us wanted to lose anyone else. None of them said anything, though, but I could see the relief of Tady's and Bair's faces. They hadn't yet mastered the art of the blank face. I wasn't sure if that was a good or bad thing. One thing I did know, neither of them were going to accompany me into the shed. Killing demons was one thing. Torture was something else. I'd been telling the truth when I'd said demons weren't humans, but inflicting pain on something, no matter how evil, took a person someplace dark. Best to keep innocent – relatively so anyway – as long as possible.

I looked at Kassia and Fynn. Annabella wasn't going to be happy, but it had been their capture. Besides, a reminder I was in charge never hurt, especially after my close call.

"Kassia, Fynn. With me."

I caught Annabella's scowl, but Grady put his hand on her arm and she settled almost immediately. The pull I'd felt towards Tempest twisted with a longing I hadn't felt in years, or at least one I hadn't admitted to since I'd first received the power. I wanted to be bonded. Only now, it wasn't some vague feeling that I wanted to be bonded to some nameless, unknown person.

It was Tempest. I wanted that connection with her.

Only her.

I shut down that train of thought as the four of us walked towards the shed. I couldn't be thinking anything remotely emotional when I did this. The Qaniss were ruthless warriors, Adonai's chosen ones, but I had to go a step further than I would have in a battle. If I lost control in there, I wasn't only in danger of killing the demon. The energy flowing through me could burst out, and that kind of damage could be catastrophic.

I didn't have time to siphon off the excess. While I intended to do most of the work, I needed a bonded pair nearby in case it became too dangerous for me to continue.

"Have you done this before?" Tempest asked.

I wasn't sure which of us she was talking to, but I answered anyway, "Yes. Personally, twice. I've watched a couple others though. The Council oversaw interrogations, and then provided the rest of us with the information we needed."

I tried not to think of my father, but I couldn't stop the flashes of memory. Of him standing in front of an *excoriator*, trying to make sense out of its hissings. Watching him peel away the skin of a *ardens lingua*, while being careful not to get any of its blood on his skin. Taking the wings from a *beach cliseadh*. I'd first practiced on one of those.

"Nice people you had back home. Teaching kids how to torture."

"You'll want to stay quiet about things you don't understand." Kassia's voice was soft.

I stiffened, waiting for another smart remark from Tempest, but she didn't say anything. I didn't know why, but I was glad. I didn't think I could handle an argument between her and Kassia at the moment. Kassia was fairly even-tempered and Fynn was easy-going, but I knew neither of them would take kindly to disparaging remarks about home. The

Qaniss weren't perfect, but the loss of our world was still too fresh to take criticism about our ways.

I stepped over the marks Annabella had made and motioned for Tempest to do the same. I hadn't explained their meaning to her, but she followed my example without question. A glance at her showed her expression was serious, as if she could feel the weight about what we were going to do. Perhaps she could. I certainly did.

The *spinis* looked up when we opened the door to the shed, its lizard-like face full of contempt and hate. Its tongue flicked out, tasting the air, and its yellow-green widened slightly. I wondered if it could taste the extra energy inside me, or if it could sense something different from Tempest.

"Qaniss."

All demons had a little bit of a hissing sound. Well, except the *vihane surma*. They didn't speak. No mouths. We never bothered to capture them.

"Why you no kill me?"

At least this one spoke English. My aptitude for languages extended to the demonic, of course. Tempest, however, wouldn't have had a chance to learn any demonic tongue and she needed to hear what this creature had to say, especially if she was going to understand why I had to do what came next.

"We need information," I said. "And you're going to give it

to us."

The *spinis* spit onto the floor. "You kill me first."

"No." I shook my head. "I will kill you, but not first. You will talk."

I walked towards it, my steps slow and even. Kassia and Fynn had broken off a few of the spikes on its hands and the thick black ichor that was demon blood oozed over the chains Kassia had used to bind it. I almost thought to ask her where she'd gotten them, but I didn't. It wasn't important at the moment. I trusted that she and Annabella had put enough power into them to hold the *spinis* until I was done.

"Those look like they hurt." I gestured towards his hands. One of the large spines on its back had been broken as well. "In fact, I know they do. *Spinis* have nerves running through their spikes. Demon anatomy 101. They're not just bone."

I heard Tempest make a noise behind me, and I knew she'd understood what I was going to do. I didn't look at her, not even when I saw the demon's eyes flick towards her and back again.

"You let him hurt me?"

"Don't talk to her," I snapped. Its eyes narrowed and I knew I'd made a mistake. "You talk to me."

"You are young." Its voice took on a slightly coy sound. "Too young for torture."

I reached out and put my first two fingers on one of the broken spines. It hissed from the pressure.

"Do you know who I am?" I asked.

"All Qaniss look same."

I kept my voice even. "I am Bram Robert Grimm, only living descendant of Wilhelm Grimm, the oldest of the founding families. Only son of the Council leader, Abraham Jakob Grimm." I dug my finger into the raw stump. "And you will answer my questions."

****

I handed Kassia back her blade without a word and walked out of the shed. She and Fynn would deal with the remains. I didn't look at Tempest as I passed, not wanting to see the look on her face. In the end, I'd killed the demon, but it had talked before I'd driven Kassia's knife into its heart. That was what I needed to focus on, the information it had given up, not the way it had felt hacking off its spines, digging the point of the knife into the remaining stumps, slicing off its fingers...

It hadn't screamed. Most demons didn't. But there'd been no mistaking the pain it had been in. I wondered sometimes if they'd realized what they'd gotten themselves into when they'd chosen to follow Lucifer. For them, death wouldn't be a relief, not like the Qaniss who knew that if they were being tortured, it would eventually end and they would be in paradise. No more pain. For the demons, the pain here was only the beginning of their torment.

I knew better than to feel sorry for them – they'd made their choice, after all – but I couldn't help but wonder sometimes what it must have been like. When the choice had been made. When they'd fallen from angel to demon.

I supposed, now that I thought about it, Viator and the other angels were the only other beings who could, in some small way, appreciate what the others and I were going through. In one fell swoop, they'd lost one third of their family. Though they hadn't lost everyone, what had happened to them during the fall had to have been so much worse. We had hope we would see our loved ones again. We knew they were at peace. There was no such comfort for Viator and the angels. I didn't know if they felt as humans did, but if they did, it must have been awful to have to fight against family with the knowledge of what would happen at the end.

Letting my thoughts wander for a bit as I walked had done me some good. That and the cool early morning air cleared my head. I hadn't realized we'd been in there essentially all night. When I stopped at the edge of the clearing, I found myself able to focus on the information I'd gotten.

The demons were indeed running rampant now that our

world was gone, spreading themselves out over the other worlds to attack with a vengeance. Soon, there would be a calculated attack on another world, in a place called Wycliffe, Ohio.

And I knew what that meant. If Tempest was to go with us, I would need to bond with her, no matter what the consequences were for me.

Chapter Seventeen

Tempest

I waited until Bram had gone a few feet before I walked out of the shed as well. It didn't look like Kassia and Fynn needed me to stay and help with whatever they were going to do, but I wasn't about to ask. I didn't want to talk to any of them ever again, especially not Bram, not after what I'd seen him do.

The thing – the demon – had looked more like a lizard than a human. A talking lizard that could stand on two feet and had hands like a person. Well, except for the whole spiny knuckles thing. I'd watched enough sci-fi though to have a hard time seeing something that could speak as not being on the same level as a human. I supposed it looked like some sort of alien to me, especially with the black blood, but I was having a hard time seeing it as evil.

Then it had talked to me.

Dimly, I'd been aware of Bram telling it to leave me alone, to talk to him, but I hadn't really been paying attention to the conversation. All I'd been able think about had been the cold, wet sensation that had run over and through me when it had spoken. I'd never felt anything like it. I'd known, in that moment I knew, Bram had been telling the truth.

It wasn't human. It wasn't some science fiction extra-terrestrial. There was no good in these things. They were evil. Evil in a way I'd never understood evil before.

A memory came to me then, a memory I hadn't thought of in a long time.

****

He glared down at me, lips twitching with anger. I'd known better than to mouth off to Father Russ, but I'd done it anyway. I hated him. Hated the way he looked at me. He'd told me more than once that I had the devil inside me, an evil that couldn't be tamed, but must be exorcised. The foster family I'd been living with for the past six weeks hadn't believed him...until now.

I'd made the mistake of protesting the dress code Father Russ had given, and not just protesting, but giving him a few choice words regarding his accompanying sermon about sinful women and their temptation of the male gender. Apparently, that had been enough to convince my foster parents I needed an exorcism.

He splashed more holy water in my face and began another string of Latin. The room was hot and I was soaked with sweat. He had some sort of incense burning, something thick and cloying that made me want to sneeze and cough and choke all at the same time. I wasn't sure if that's what was supposed to get rid of the demon inside me, but I supposed if it was living in my lungs, it would've wanted out by now.

The thought made me laugh, which made me cough, then laugh even harder. I could see my foster parents out of the corner of my eye, horror on their faces, and I knew I'd be heading back to the group home, probably first thing in the morning. It was just as well, I supposed. I'd felt like the foster family had taken me not despite my juvie record, but because of it, like they thought it was their Christian duty to save me. Now I was sure that's what they'd been thinking, and they'd come away tonight knowing they'd failed.

****

I almost wanted to smile. I wondered what Father Russ would say if he could see me now, battling against true demons, if he heard I'd apparently been chosen by God. He wouldn't believe it, I knew. He'd been thoroughly convinced of my villainy. And I'd only been eleven at the time.

Movement by the cabin caught my eye and I saw Annabella standing in the doorway. I would've known it was her even if I hadn't seen Grady at her side. The Poe twins might've been identical for the most part, but I was starting to be able to tell the difference. For one thing, Leigh didn't tend to look at me with quite so much...dislike didn't seem like a strong enough word, but it wasn't quite hatred. Maybe loathing was more accurate. I didn't really understand what Annabella's problem was, but I knew animosity when I felt it.

I looked away from her and saw Bram standing at the end of the clearing. I'd been walking towards him without even realizing it. I frowned. I didn't want this. I'd made my peace long ago with being on my own. I preferred it now. No one to be accountable to or to worry about. It was only me and I liked it that way.

But I still kept walking. I was a bit surprised I could actually see him considering dawn was still a few hours away, but my night vision had always been good. I made a face. I supposed now I knew why.

When I reached him, I didn't say anything. What could I say to someone I'd watched torture a demon? It wasn't really the torture that was bothering me though. As soon as the demon had talked to me, I'd known it for what it was. What I was having a hard time dealing with was the blank expression Bram had worn the entire time he was doing those horrible things.

"'We shall see that at which dogs howl in the dark, and at which cats prick up their ears after midnight.'" Bram's voice was soft.

I recognized the quote. "Lovecraft?"

He gave me a surprised glance.

"I may have a questionable past," I said. "But I'm quite well-read."

He returned his attention to whatever it was he'd been looking at before. "Lovecraft was one of us," he said. "And that's what we do. We're the ones who see the evil, the ones who stand between the worlds and the darkness."

"No matter what it takes?" I asked.

Bram's bloody hands closed into fists, but I still saw the faint tremble. "Whatever Adonai puts before us."

I looked down at my hands. They were clean, but they didn't feel that way.

"How many others?" I asked. It wasn't the first time the question had occurred to me, but the first time I'd thought to ask it, though it was more for distraction than anything else.

"Others?"

"Everyone's last names, they're all writers, poets. You said Shakespeare and Lovecraft were Qaniss." I was still trying to wrap my head around that one. "Are the other last names, are they referring to the people I think they are?"

Bram nodded. "Shakespeare was the original, but Wilhelm Grimm's line has been considered the oldest since Shakespeare had no descendants." He glanced at me. "Until now."

Right. The author of *Hamlet* and *Romeo and Juliet* was my grandfather. My high school English teachers would've loved this. "So the Grimm brothers...?"

"Wilhelm was Qaniss. His brother was not. As far as we know, Jakob didn't know Wilhelm coded their work."

"Coded?"

"Throughout the worlds, the greatest of the Qaniss used their talent to hand down information from generation to generation."

"Who else?" I asked. I noticed Bram seemed a bit more solid now that he was talking about history rather than what had happened. That was good. I was starting to feel more calm myself.

"Edgar Allen Poe."

With the twins, that wasn't much of a surprise.

"Hans Christian Anderson. Charlotte and Emily Bronte. Lewis Carroll."

That one surprised me a bit. I'd always found his work a bit creepy, though I guessed if I'd suddenly been given some divine calling, and asked to write stories to transcend worlds, I might be a bit out there too.

"HG Wells. Jane Austen."

I almost smirked at the idea of Austen and the Bronte sisters being warriors. I'd never been a fan of their works.

Romance novels, had never really been my thing. I didn't laugh though. I may not know exactly what I thought of this whole thing, but I wouldn't be disrespectful.

"Bram Stoker." He gave me a half-smile. "And before you ask, no, I'm not related. My father's bonded was. Lucan's father."

I saw a brief shadow of grief cross his face and my heart twisted in sympathy. And something else.

"Mary Shelley. Mark Twain. Charles Dickens." He sounded like he was rushing to finish now. "Jules Verne, Samuel Taylor Coleridge and Robert Frost."

"That's quite a list," I said. "Sounds like half of my required reading in high school." I raised an eyebrow. "Does that mean I already know the secret handshake?" I asked.

"You'll learn interpretation later," he said, expression back to being unreadable.

"All right," I said. "Then what do we do now?"

"The demon said they were planning on attacking Wycliffe, Ohio," he said. "So we protect it."

My stomach lurched, all semblance of calm gone. "I'm from Wycliffe."

He looked at me sharply. "What?"

I met his eyes. "That's where I grew up. Wycliffe, Ohio." A thought hit me. "Could they...could they be looking for me?"

I saw him start, his mask slipping for a moment. There was shock, and something else, something darker. A thrill ran through me. I'd never had anyone look at me like that before, like he would throw himself in harm's way to protect me. I swallowed hard and looked away. He'd already done that.

"It's possible," he admitted. "We don't know how much they know about the prophecy." He sighed and turned towards me. "But no matter what the reason is, we need to go."

I nodded.

"And that means it's time."

I didn't like the way that sounded.

"They aren't attacking here, Tempest. They're attacking in another world."

Okay, so maybe I was a bit slow on the uptake, but I finally got it. "I can't travel between worlds," I said. I was surprised at how much the idea of them leaving bothered me. I couldn't even imagine Bram leaving me. It didn't seem possible. The connection between us would snap, and neither one of us could let that happen.

"You can," he said. His face was tight, eyes hard, as if this was the last thing he wanted. "Once we bond."

"Bond," I echoed. "You and me?"

"I know Tady told you," he said softly. "About me. How I

never bonded, but I received Adonai's power anyway."

I flushed, but lifted my chin. "I deserved to know if I'm a Qaniss."

"You did," he agreed. "It's just...it's not an easy thing for me to talk about."

I could tell he was still hiding something, but I didn't ask. Bram was the kind of man who would bury things deeper if I tried to pry.

"You're a smart person, Tempest."

He looked directly at me, the expression on his face clearly saying he'd rather be looking anywhere else. Something inside me fluttered.

"I know you've figured it out," he continued. "What you are to...what we are to each other."

After a moment's hesitation, I nodded. The air grew thick between us, around us. I could feel something humming, like the electricity filling the air after an electrical storm. "We're bonded. Or, we were supposed to be?"

He nodded. "Some Qaniss believe the reason some of us don't have a bonded is because the bonded either died in childhood or was never born for some reason."

"Or they were born in another world?" I tried to make it light, but my attempt fell flat.

"You're two years younger than me," he said.

I wasn't sure what that meant, but I waited. I had no doubt he'd explain.

"I don't think it's a coincidence you received the tattoo when you were ten," he said. He reached his hand out, but didn't quite touch the mark on my wrist. "Because I was twelve. I would even wager that your birthday is in April."

"The twelfth," I said.

"Mine is the fourteenth."

"I got the tattoo two days after my birthday," I said slowly. This was too much. Things didn't happen like that. I didn't believe in fate or destiny, no matter what crazy stuff I'd seen recently. And more important... "I don't believe in God."

His eyes narrowed and I almost squirmed. He looked like he was trying to see inside me, and I remembered how Tady had said bonded people could communicate telepathically. I hoped that only applied to people who'd actually gone through whatever ritual or process they needed.

"Why did you choose a cross?"

I hadn't been expecting that question. I'd thought he'd react in anger, disbelief. Argue with me. Not something matter-of-fact and logical. People who believed in a Creator, an all-knowing Being, God, they weren't supposed to be calm when their beliefs were questioned.

"I don't know," I admitted. I couldn't remember what had

drawn me to this particular design.

"I do," he said. His gaze was steady. "You may not believe in Adonai, but He believes in you. He chose you for this purpose." He paused for a moment before adding, "But it is your choice."

"My choice to believe or my choice to bond with you?" I asked.

"Both," he answered. "But I don't think belief is actually the problem. Not belief in Adonai's existence anyway."

"Really?" I folded my arms, a challenge in the word. A challenge for him to say what he thought he knew about me.

"You stayed," he said. "Despite your insistence that we're crazy, and might even be dangerous, you didn't run. You might not be ready to admit it to yourself, but you believe God exists. Your problem is, you don't think He cares."

Chapter Eighteen

Bram

I was right and I knew she knew it. I also knew she wasn't about to admit it. The thing was, I didn't know what to do. With very few exceptions, Qaniss readily accepted the reality of Adonai, as well as His role in our lives. Even the ones who used their power for nefarious purposes didn't deny Adonai's existence.

The Qaniss who married outside our people were generally led to other believers, ones who would, while unable to fight themselves, raise their children in the faith. In all our history, I could think of only a handful of Qaniss who had chosen to leave either due to their own unbelief or that of their partner.

If Tempest didn't believe, how could we even bond to begin with? Though, if that was the case, how did she even have any of Adonai's power to begin with? And I knew she had it. She'd healed me, and it hadn't been demonic power pretending to be something else. I knew the difference.

It was impossible to bond with someone who didn't believe. If one of a bonded pair decided they no longer believed, the power was lost. It was the only way to break a bond aside from death, and the only way both didn't die, because they both lost the power. The one who still believed became like a Qaniss who'd never bonded.

Trust me.

I started. I knew that voice. Every Qaniss did. But it had been a long time since I'd heard Him so clearly.

Bond with her.

I mentally argued back. *You know what will happen if I do. I can't go back.*

I have chosen you and her for this purpose. Will you refuse to obey My will?

And that was the question now, I knew. It was no longer about Tempest and what she believed, but rather whether or not I was going to be obedient.

Some people assumed, if someone heard clear directions from Adonai, it made following those directions easier. I knew from experience that wasn't the case. I'd made my fair share of mistakes over the years, but when it came to the decisions I knew Adonai wanted me to make, I'd been obedient. For the first time in my life, I wanted to refuse.

I wasn't afraid the bonding wouldn't work. I was scared it would. And scared was the right word, no matter how much I hated it. I'd grown up knowing what it meant to be bonded, preparing myself to become half of a whole, to have someone know me better than I knew myself.

And then I'd realized it wasn't going to happen.

I'd struggled for a while, and the only way I'd been able to come to grips with it had been to isolate myself, retreat inward. I didn't have anyone to share the power with, no one to help me carry the burden. It was only me, and I'd accepted it would always be that way.

Now, I had to change all of that. I could already feel some of the changes. I was more aware of Tempest, where she was, how she felt, than I was of the others. Once we bonded, it would only become more intense. We would be able to take each other's pain, speak into each other's minds.

That, we would both have. But the secret I'd been keeping from her, and from the others, meant there was one part of the bond that would be different for her than it would be for me. I could still hear the Seer, her ancient voice cracking as her unseeing eyes had stared off into space.

"I have a word from Shadday. He bids me tell you that your chosen will come to you and you will know her by the mark she bears. She will wear her lineage on her skin, but know it not. She will come from a house that has been lost. She will be either your salvation or your undoing, but you will be bound to her heart and soul, even if she takes your life."

Only now did I realize the Seer had used a name of Adonai's that meant "the storm of God." That wouldn't have made any sense to me then, but I hadn't put much store in the prophecy. I knew our history and only one house had been considered lost. I hadn't exactly dismissed the Seer's prophecy, but I'd considered it more to be an attempt to put her into my father's good graces. I'd been fifteen and knew that my lack of romantic interest in anyone had concerned my father since I'd been the only one left in the direct Grimm family line.

When I'd realized Tempest was the missing Qaniss, I'd tried very hard not to think about the words of either prophecy, but once I'd seen the Shakespeare quote tattooed on her collarbone, I'd known that I couldn't deny it. The Seer's words had come back to me then: *"she will wear her lineage on her skin, but know it not."*

I could feel the love bond pulling me towards Tempest as strongly as my power called to hers, and I knew if I bonded with her, my half of the love bond would be woven into our bond, linking me forever with her. It wouldn't only mean I couldn't fall in love with anyone else, but rather that, no matter what choice Tempest made, I would love her forever. There would be no moving on, no getting over her. It would be permanent and always.

But I knew what I had to do.

"We don't have a lot of time." I couldn't look at her, not when she held so much of me in her hands. "You have to make your choice."

"There's no going back if I agree, is there?"

Her voice was solid, but I could feel the anxiety radiating off of her. Even if we hadn't been connected, I knew I'd have been able to feel it. Still, I answered honestly. I wouldn't tell her about the other thing. That was mine alone to bear, but I would be honest with her about the rest.

"If you deny Adonai, we lose our power, but you go free. That's the only way short of death."

I heard her mutter something under her breath about me being melodramatic, but I didn't argue that I was serious. She hadn't been raised Qaniss. She didn't understand.

"The power I felt," she spoke quietly, but I had no problem hearing her. "That comes from your...our God? Adonai?"

"That's what we call Him most of the time, yes."

"If I'd only heard about it, I could think you were crazy." She sighed. "But I felt it, and I can't deny it. I suppose I could try to explain it away somehow, but..."

Her voice trailed off and I risked a glance at her. The sun was starting to set and her face was shadowed, hiding the scar on her cheek. I felt a jolt of pain and anger as I wondered who had hurt her.

"Once you've felt real power," I said. "It's hard to deny where it comes from."

She gave me a sharp look and I knew I'd put into words

what she hadn't been able to say.

"Is that enough?" She turned towards me, jade eyes glittering. "Is it enough for me to acknowledge where it comes from? I don't have the faith you do."

I didn't answer right away, listening for my own answer. It came quickly.

Trust me.

"For now," I said. "At some point, Adonai will expect you to make a commitment." I took a slow breath. "But for now, He will honor what you offer."

I saw her working things over in her mind and I stayed silent. The choice had to be hers.

Finally, she spoke, "My whole life, I've listened to my gut." She looked at me. "And now it's telling me this is what I'm supposed to do."

I didn't tell her it was Adonai, not her gut, speaking to her. That was something she'd come to accept or deny on her own.

"Am I going to get..." Her voice trailed off and when her eyes flicked over my shoulder, I knew what she was asking.

"Wings?" I supplied the word.

She nodded mutely.

"I don't know," I answered honestly. "No one's ever bonded like this before. But you should be prepared. If it happens, it's going to hurt."

She gave me a grim look. "I've dealt with pain before."

I didn't contradict her, but I knew it wouldn't be the same. I'd barely kept from passing out when I'd gotten mine. Even with all of my other injuries over the years, I'd never felt anything else like it.

"So it's the power to fight demons, the ability to travel between worlds, and maybe wings." She looked down at her hands. "Or staying here and being on my own again."

"Are you agreeing to bond with me?" I asked the question flat-out, needing her to say it now that she knew the cost.

She lifted her chin, letting her eyes meet mine. "I am."

I nodded, fighting not to show how much her decision meant to me. "All right. We'll need the others to witness."

"Witness?"

She sounded nervous and I wondered if it was more at the idea of people watching than the actual ritual itself.

"This isn't just some sort of commitment between the two of us." I managed not to flinch at my word choice.

She could never know what this had to be for me. She would never forgive me.

I finished answering her question. "You're acknowledging before Adonai, and the rest of the Qaniss that you are accepting His power and the responsibility of protecting all realms from the forces of darkness." I forced myself to speak around the lump in my throat. "As we are all who remain, it is our duty to bear witness."

"Bram," Lucan's voice interrupted and both of us turned to look at him. "Kassia and Fynn told us what the demon said. When are we leaving?"

I nodded. "Soon." I didn't look at Tempest as I added, "But first, there's something we need to do. Ask the rest to come out here. And bring your knife."

I caught a faint look of surprise, but then it was gone and he was heading back to the cabin.

"What does he need a knife for?" Tempest's voice was hard.

"There's blood when you get a tattoo," I said, watching Lucan walk away. "It's part of the ritual. Since we already have the marks, we need to get the blood another way."

"Great," she muttered.

I half-expected her to argue, but she didn't. I had to admit, I was more than a little surprised she'd come so far in such a short time, but I supposed when faced with the reality of the demons she'd seen and power she'd felt, she hadn't had much of a choice. Then again, I reminded myself, there were those who had seen Adonai and still refused to believe.

I pushed those thoughts aside as the others came out of the cabin. They'd cleaned up after the fight, I saw, and I was suddenly conscious of the blood, both demon and my own, covering me. I at least needed to wash my hands. I started to excuse myself, but then Tady handed me a wet towel and I was able to scrub most of the nastiness off of my hands and arms. The rest could wait until after. If anything, it'd give me an excuse to leave as soon as the ceremony was completed.

I had a feeling I wasn't going to want to be around anyone when we were finished.

"Lucan," I said as I handed the towel back to Tady. "As the second eldest, would you and your bonded consent to bond Tempest and myself?"

I felt the ripple of surprise go through the group and caught Tempest's response out of the corner of my eye. Her hands were clenched into fists, her jaw set. She looked more like she was getting ready to hit someone than to bond with me.

I felt a sudden pang for what might have been. We should have been bonded as children, grown up together with the love bond clear between us both. This should have been a formal declaration of our love bond, now she was seventeen. But, I reminded myself, if her mother hadn't been taken, if Tempest had been born on our world, she would have died centuries before my own birth. This truly was the only way the two of us ever would have met.

Trust me.

It was nothing more than a pair of whispered words, but they calmed me enough to turn towards Tempest. After a moment, she did the same, though she didn't meet my eyes.

Lucan and Annabella came and stood on the other side of Tempest and myself so they were facing the others. Lucan looked at me.

"*Je suis prest*," I said softly. Or, at least, I was as ready as I was ever going to be.

Annabella opened the ceremony with the traditional words. "'Though this be madness, yet there is method in it.'"

I caught the glimmer of recognition on Tempest's face.

Lucan continued with a line by Frost, "'They cannot scare me with their empty spaces between stars – on stars where no human race is. I have it in me so much nearer home to scare myself with my own desert places.'"

Annabella picked up the next part perfectly. "A Qaniss bond is to ensure that none face the empty spaces, whether between stars or within our own desert places, alone."

Lucan looked at me. We were at the place where, normally, the two bonded would put their wrists next to each other and receive their tattoos, the blood mingling a bit before the marks were finished, and then the wrists would be placed together, crosses pressed together to complete the sharing.

"Your knife," I said quietly.

Lucan pulled it out and I held out my arm. Tempest did the same without being prompted. I could feel the power humming between our skin and one look at her face told me she felt it too.

No one had ever done this before, so I was trusting the instructions I was about to give were coming from Adonai, because if they weren't, we were going to have a problem.

"Trace the crosses," I said. "Hard enough to draw blood."

Lucan didn't question me as he started with me. I kept my eyes on Tempest as the tip of the knife cut through my skin. A memory hit me, as clear as the day it had happened, shaking me to my core.

I never talked about that day and I tried not to think about it, but I knew I'd never realized this before.

I'd been thinking of her.

When I'd been receiving the tattoo, feeling Adonai's power coursing through me, I'd had a vision. There was no other word for it, because I couldn't have known who she was at the time. It didn't matter that I'd never seen Tempest as a child, I knew now it had been her face in my mind, keeping me sane. Her hair had been a bit longer, her face still slightly rounded in childhood, and the scar on her cheek had been newer, but was even more of a confirmation of her identity.

I'd seen her getting her mark.

I could feel the blood dripping down my wrist as Lucan finished and then started on Tempest. Her eyes jerked towards me the moment the knife touched her and our gazes locked. I couldn't read her mind, but in that moment, I could feel the same sort of shock run through her, and I wondered if, she too, had remembered something she'd forgotten these past seven years.

Lucan finished and handed his knife to Annabella. He took my arm and turned it over so my wrist rested on Tempest's, though I kept my wrist slightly bent to keep the marks from pressing together. There was one more thing to say before that happened. I wrapped my fingers around her forearm and she did the same.

"Repeat after me," I said quietly. We were supposed to say it together, but she wouldn't know the words. "'Tree at my window, window tree...'"

She said the words, then joined me as I continued the quote, our voice blending together. "'My sash is lowered when night comes on; / But let there never be curtain drawn / Between you and me.'"

As I said the final word, I straightened my wrist and the crosses touched, our blood mingling, and the power began to flow. Tempest's nails dug into my arm and I could hear her gasping for air. With a start, I realized I could feel her heart beating, hear the blood in her veins. I could feel every inch of her, the rough patches of scar tissue, the strong, firm muscles under her skin. Her eyes were glowing and I found myself lost in them.

I'd always considered myself a whole person, but I knew now that had been a lie. There had been empty spaces all throughout me and she filled them even as I felt myself doing the same for her. Only now could I truly appreciate the miracle it had taken to bring us together.

And there, beneath all of that, was something still broken, still not whole.

I loved her.

So much of who she was remained a mystery, but none of that mattered.

I could see her.

Not her physical appearance, though I found her attractive as well, but her soul. This wasn't an ordinary sort of love, the kind that grew over time or even the head-spinning sort of passion that some experienced with a physical attraction. This was something reserved for only a few. A complete, unconditional love that only Adonai could provide.

That was how I loved her, would always love her, even if she never returned it.

Her hand released me and I let go as well, barely hearing

Tady chattering on about how amazing the ritual had been. I needed to be alone. I couldn't look at Tempest anymore, not without her seeing that something was wrong. And I couldn't tell her.

She could never know.

Chapter Nineteen

Tempest

The bandage on my wrist itched, but I resisted the urge to scratch. It was surprisingly easy since I had all of this insane power coursing through my body to distract me. My brain was working overtime, my thoughts bouncing from one thing to another. I'd always had a hard time concentrating – hence the ADHD diagnosis – but all of this energy made it so much worse.

I'd thought I'd felt things before, little jolts of power, and then there'd been the two times I'd touched Bram...I pushed those thoughts aside. I didn't want to think about Bram. I wanted to think about the power I had and what it meant.

I remembered what Bram had said when we'd been training. More specifically, when we'd been running. He'd been crazy fast, faster than any human should be. Did that mean I would be the same way? Faster? Stronger? Heightened senses?

I flexed my fingers and I could feel the strength in them.

I'd never have to worry about someone hurting me again. Sure, these guys were just as strong and they could fight better, and there were the demons, but regular people? They wouldn't stand a chance.

I'd told Bram the truth when I'd said I'd learned to fight out of necessity. Even that hadn't always been enough though. It couldn't stop the ones who'd been bigger than me, weighed more. I could feel my chest tightening at the memory of a heavy body on me, pinning me down...

Pain ripped through me and I fell to my knees. I gritted my teeth together as I felt the skin on my back begin to tear. It was a familiar sensation, though more intense than anything I'd ever felt before. I squeezed my eyes closed and dug my fingers into the dirt, refusing to scream. I wasn't even sure I could've managed a sound since I couldn't even breathe.

And then it was gone as quickly as it had come. I let out a shaky breath and felt something new move with my ribs as I exhaled. I raised my head and saw what I'd known would be there. What I could see was jade green, like my eyes, streaked with a deep rich brown. They shook out and I felt them stretch. I stood carefully, my body adjusting to the new weight with more ease than I'd expected. It almost felt as if I'd been off-balance before, and this was how my body had always been meant to move. I looked from one to the other, estimating my wingspan was at least two inches longer than my five feet, five inches of height.

I had wings.

"Tempest."

I turned to see Tady looking up at me.

"Your wings are beautiful." She smiled at me, but I could see concern in her eyes.

 With a start, I realized the other Qaniss had vanished, most likely to do whatever they needed to do to prepare for our little trip. Well, all of them except Bair. He was lingering a few yards away, probably in an attempt to act like he was giving us some privacy. I didn't doubt he could still hear us anyway. I got it now though, why he didn't go too far. Aside from the fact that he was clearly in love with Tady. I wondered if she saw it, but then dismissed the thought. It wasn't any of my business. No, my business was...

I frowned. Where had Bram gone?

As soon as I thought it, I felt a familiar tug inside me, the same kind of tug that had brought me from Ohio to Colorado. It was stronger now and, even though I could recognize it, there was something different about it. I wasn't exactly sure how to describe it, only that it almost felt as if there were some sort of cord connecting me to Bram, one I could follow, mentally or physically, to find him wherever he was.

"Are ye okay?" Tady put her hand on my arm.

I jerked away at the touch, wings twitching. "Sorry," I muttered. "Not much of a touchy type person."

She gave me a smile that said her feelings weren't hurt. She was definitely the easiest one of the group to get along with. I wondered how old she was. She barely looked older than thirteen or fourteen, though I suspected she was at least a couple years older than that. At least, I hoped she was.

"We need to start packin' and preparin' to go." She looked at the rising sun. "We'll want to get some rest tonight so we can leave at first light in the morn. We dinna want to get caught at night in an unscouted location."

"We'll be in Wycliffe, right?" I said, trying to ignore the persistent nagging thought that I was too far away from Bram, that I needed to get closer. I hadn't counted on that. "It's not a big city, but it's not like we'll be exactly in the middle of nowhere."

"We'll be comin' into the other world at the same coordinates where we left this one," Tady said.

Curiosity was enough to distract me, the way learning something new had always helped me cope with pain and discomfort. I wasn't only well-read, multi-lingual and one of the best hackers in the country because I was smart. I'd had a lot of things growing up I'd needed to be distracted from.

"Why don't we just go straight there from here?" I asked.

"When ye travel for the first time, ye will ken it better," she said. "But, simply put, it's hard enough movin' from world to world. Tryin' to move to a different place at the same time..." She shook her head. "As far as I ken, no one's ever done it. We're taught not to even try."

I wondered if the Qaniss always did what they were told, but I didn't ask. I didn't want to bring up memories of a world that didn't exist anymore. I'd never had anything to lose, so it was hard for me to truly understand what they were going through, but I could only imagine how horrible it must be to have everything, a family, a home, people who loved you, and then lose everything all at once. Almost everything, I amended, they all had their bonded.

Except Bram. The bond pulsed inside me, strong enough to make me catch my breath. Bram had lost everything from his world. He had the others, but even in the short time I'd been with them, I'd seen he held himself apart from them.

That, I understood. If there'd been a degree offered in being aloof, I would've gotten a Ph.D years ago. Now, though, I wasn't alone, and it was the strangest feeling, knowing there was this permanent connection to another person.

"Ye should fetch Bram," Tady said.

"Me?" I didn't try to hide my surprise.

"Aye." Her expression was serious, but I caught a hint of humor in her eyes.

I suspected I was going to be getting a lot of that. The new girl who didn't know how things worked. Oh goody.

"You know him better than I do," I argued. I pulled my wings in. I wondered if they were invisible now because even though I could feel them, I could also feel my shirt against my skin. I could see how people would be fascinated by how that worked.

Now she did smile, but it was a kind one. "It doesna matter. Even if Bram had his kin here, ye would still be the one to fetch him." She glanced over her shoulder at the cabin, her gaze lingering on Bair for a moment before it came back to me. "Annabella and Leigh are the only two who I've ever seen have a connection with each other almost as deep as with their bonded." She opened her mouth like she was going to say something, then closed it again.

"What?" I could see the debate in her eyes. There was something she wanted to tell me, but wasn't sure how. "Just say it."

"Did Bram tell ye that some Qaniss have gifts?" Her cheeks went pink, but there was a stubborn light in her eyes I liked. It said she'd made up her mind and she was going to go through with it.

"He said you..." I hesitated, then amended what I'd said. "He said *we* were faster and stronger than other people. And, you know, we can fly."

"Aye, all that's true enough," Tady agreed. "But that's not

what I mean. Every Qaniss has enhanced senses, things like that, but I'm talkin' about gifts, like Lucan's healing. It's not like he kin lay hands on someone, and they're magically healed, but it's a bit more than just havin' a knack for somethin'. A bit of his power's about the healin'."

"Okay." I wasn't sure where this was going, but I didn't doubt Tady had a point.

"I have a gift." She lifted her chin, as if expecting me to argue. "I...ken things. *Know* them. Not like seein' the future or readin' minds or anything like that. I get these strong impressions sometimes. Feelin's about certain things."

"So, psychic?" I tried not to sound skeptical. After everything I'd seen recently, I wasn't sure why I'd find it hard to believe something else supernatural.

"No." She shook her head. "It's almost impossible to explain. Like tryin' to tell someone what it feels like to bond." She gestured towards my bandaged wrist. "Could you explain it?"

"No," I agreed. "I couldn't." I gave her a curious look. "But I don't understand why you wanted to tell me that. Right now anyway."

The blush that had faded rushed back, leaving her fair, freckled skin mottled pink and white. "I had to tell you because there is somethin' ye need to ken about the bond between ye 'n Bram."

"I know it's not a normal one," I said dismissively. "Since we weren't the right age and all."

She shook her head. "That's not what I meant. When people bond, I kin sense it. Almost see it. And there's somethin' I'm sure he dinna tell you." Her eyes met mine. "Bonded pairs, on occasion, experience a different sort of connection. It's triggered when they first bond, but manifests itself appropriately for whatever their age, growing with them, but it doesna go away. Ever. It's a love bond."

"Excuse me?" I blinked.

"A pair who are love bonded never looks at anyone else. Never wants anyone else."

"I don't understand." I shook my head. "I don't love...I mean..."

"I dinna ken how it's to work since there's never been another pair like you, but I ken what I sensed. There is more to yer bond than one between two Qaniss." Tady gave me a serious look. "I dinna ken why Bram dinna tell you, but Adonai told me ye needed to know." She gave me a nod and turned back towards Bair and the cabin.

"Thank you." I barely heard myself say the words.

A love bond? Some sort of fairytale love at first sight kind of thing? Between me and Bram? Sure, he was good-looking, and I couldn't deny I was a bit attracted to him, but love? The forever kind?

I turned towards the river, instinctively know that's where he had gone. I could feel him there. I'd go get him, but he and I were going to have a little talk before we went back to the cabin. He had some explaining to do, and if he'd done what I thought he did, I was going to test out how much new power I'd gotten from our little ritual. And he wasn't going to like it.

I tugged at the connection between us as I made my way through the underbrush, testing it. With a start, I felt Bram pull back, almost like he was replying. I knew, in theory, we were supposed to be able to talk to each other in our minds, but I wasn't going to try that. This was already weird enough without having someone else in my head.

"What's wrong?" Bram's voice was quiet as I stepped out from among the trees. He didn't turn to look at me, but I could see the tension in his body. "I felt the pain. Did you get your wings?"

I didn't say anything as I moved closer. There were a million things I wanted to say, but no idea how I was supposed to start any conversation. I flicked out my wings to answer his question, then pulled them back in. I was too angry to deal with my body's changes at the moment.

"I can feel it, Tempest," Bram said with a sigh. "You're

annoyed or angry about something. What is it?"

I folded my arms over my chest. Right. I could tell now I wasn't only seeing his tension in his body language, but sensing it as well. "Tady said there was something different about our bond."

He angled his body towards me, but didn't look at me. "We bonded later than anyone else ever has. There's nothing normal about it."

"She said she had a...gift. That she could almost see the bond."

Bram said something too quiet for me to hear, but I was pretty sure it wasn't complimentary to Tady.

"She told me about a different kind of bond some Qaniss have." I couldn't bring myself to say the 'l' word.

"She told you about love bonds," he said, his voice flat.

"Yes."

"She should've minded her own business." He threw a rock into the river with a vicious snap of his wrist.

"Is there something you need to tell me?" I shifted my weight from one foot to the other. Even though he looked calm on the outside, I could feel the turmoil inside and it fed my own anxiety.

He made a noise I interpreted to mean he didn't like my question.

Tough.

"I'm getting really tired of having to learn about things from Tady when you're supposed to be..." My voice trailed off. I knew we were connected but it was still too surreal to truly acknowledge.

"You think this is easy for me?" Bram snapped.

My eyebrows went up as he turned towards me. His eyes flashed, the mask he usually wore cracking.

"Seven years, Tempest," he continued. "I've spent seven years believing I was alone, that I had to carry this power, this responsibility, by myself. Then, two days ago, this stranger shows up, and I find out I'm not alone. That..." His hands closed into fists and I felt his struggle for control. He closed his eyes and I had the feeling he was counting to ten.

I hadn't thought about any of that, I realized as I studied his face. I hadn't stopped to consider his side of things. Surrounded by people who were paired off, and knowing they were sharing something he'd never have.

"We have no choice when it comes to love bonds, Tempest." His shoulders slumped and, when his eyes opened, they slid away from mine.

"So we...I..."

He shook his head. "I don't know how it works, so the only explanation I can offer is that Adonai always gives you a choice."

"Tady said there wasn't a choice." My heart was beating faster now.

"The choice for a Qaniss comes when they choose to bond. Every Qaniss, from the youngest to the oldest, knows about the possibility of a love bond before they're bonded. They accept it." He ran his hand through his hair.

"But I didn't know," I said.

He glanced at me, and I felt something sharp go through our connection. "No. And that's why I didn't tell you."

"You didn't want to be bonded to me." My heart twisted with a pain sharper than what I'd felt from my wings. I didn't like it. I didn't like that he could make me feel that way.

His head jerked up, eyes wide. "Don't you get it? If I would've told you, you wouldn't have bonded, which meant you couldn't travel. And we have to go. I couldn't ask the others to go without me."

"You could have gone too." I remembered how I'd felt when I'd first thought of him leaving without me. With the bond, it was worse. I couldn't imagine being far away even on the same world. I was beginning to understand why the bonded pairs were always together.

"No," he said. "I couldn't have." He looked at me now and I read more in his eyes than I wanted to.

"But you knew." I already knew the answer, but I had to hear him say it. "You knew if you bonded with me..."

"That my half of the love bond would be solidified," he finished. "Yes, I knew."

"But you did it anyway."

He met my eyes without flinching away, and his voice was firm. "Yes. I needed you. I need you."

My stomach clenched. No one needed me.

"I'm not asking you for anything beyond this bond." He took a step towards me, but kept his hands at his sides. "Being able to share the power...it's more than I thought I'd ever have."

He'd known bonding with me would mean he could never fall in love with anyone else, that he might never get anything from me beyond friendship, and he'd done it anyway. And he wasn't asking for anything in return.

I grabbed the front of his shirt and yanked him to me without stopping to consider what I was doing. He stiffened in surprise as our mouths came together, but I was the one who was caught off guard.

Electricity and fireworks and all the things I'd always made fun of people for talking about when it came to a kiss. I felt all of it. And more. It was like something deep inside me was waking up, a part of me I'd never realized existed coming to life.

Then he was pushing me away. His hands were gentle, but he was still breaking the kiss, moving me even as he took a step back. I stared at him, confused.

"I won't do this."

I blinked. "What are you talking about? You said you have this whole love bond thing with me."

"I do." He dropped his hands, but kept looking at me, his gaze steady. "I love you, Tempest, but I can't be with you. Not like this. Not when you don't understand, when you don't believe."

I went cold. Everything good I'd been feeling was gone. Was he serious? We were bonded. He said he loved me. I kissed him...

And he was rejecting me.

All of the walls I'd been starting to let down with the Qaniss, with Bram, slammed back into place.

I should've known better. It didn't matter that I was supposed to be descended from this great demon hunter slash writer, or that I was prophesied to be the chosen one or whatever. I didn't believe in his Adonai, and that was what mattered to him. Perfect Bram who'd done more than any Qaniss before him.

Of course I wasn't good enough for him.

"Tempest..." He started to reach towards me.

"Don't." I took a step back.

My wings automatically came out, flexing forward to come between me and him. I wouldn't cry. I never cried. Hadn't in years.

"Tady sent me to get you, so you should go. Your people want you. Wouldn't want to disappoint them."

I turned and walked away. I needed to be away from him. I couldn't look at him anymore.

Chapter Twenty

Bram

Her wings were beautiful, and I felt my own wanting to emerge, to reach out to her. Everything in me wanted that, wanted to touch her, hold her...

And then I felt her walls slamming back into place, cutting off the pain that had been there. It didn't matter if I could only feel a dull sort of ache instead of the sharp stab I'd felt from her the moment I'd told her I couldn't be with her. I wondered if she'd even been able to sense how much that had taken from me. I loved her, more than I loved anyone...except Adonai. He was my God, my Creator. And, still, following His command was agony.

Not yet.

Tempest had accepted her role as Qaniss, but the relationship she needed to have with Adonai was, as of yet, unfulfilled. I could feel Him telling me it wasn't time, that she needed to do this on her own first.

As I felt her push me away, it was all I could do to not take it back.

Why? I asked silently. *Why are You being so cruel?*

Silence.

Fine.

She walked away, and I knew I had to go too. Contrary to what fairy tales and romance novels portrayed, the world didn't stop for two people to have some sort of sappy heart-to-heart, full of flowery prose. What I felt for her wasn't like that anyway. It wasn't flowers and chocolates.

I'd never really thought about romance, and even the love bond hadn't changed that. I wasn't about to start quoting poetry or making outrageous declarations. I wanted to take care of her and protect her, but not because I thought she was fragile. I wanted her to fight at my side, but I would die to keep her safe. I saw her as she was. A warrior, like me, even if she didn't completely accept it yet.

Knowing I'd hurt her made going back to the cabin ten times harder. I didn't want to have to spend the day planning for our journey tomorrow. I wanted to go after Tempest and try to make her understand. But I knew that would be pointless. Without Adonai, comprehension was impossible. It would be like trying to explain senses to those without them. You could try by using comparisons, red to heat, blue to cold or vice versa, but there would always be some element missing. Some little bit that could only be experienced with the right sense.

I waited for something, some reassurance from Adonai that I'd done the right thing, that I wasn't supposed to go after her.

Nothing.

I sighed. Apparently, we were back to silence again.

I understood the concept of faith, the whole believing without needing to see, but there were times when a little reassurance would've been nice.

I gave myself a mental shake. I didn't have the time for this. I might not have wanted to be in charge, but I'd taken on the responsibility, and there was no going back because it got difficult.

As I walked back through the woods towards the cabin, a lump formed in my throat as I thought about my dad, wishing he was here for me to talk to, to give me advice. Advice on how to lead, on what to do about Tempest. Then again, even he couldn't have completely understood what I was going through with that last one. He'd loved my mother very much, but as strong as their love had been, it hadn't been the same.

My grandparents had, however, been love bonded, and I had vague memories of watching them together. They'd been among some of the oldest of all the Qaniss when they'd finally passed away. After having been bonded at the age of eight, they'd had their love bonding ceremony performed when they'd turned seventeen. After fifty-two years of marriage, they'd died within minutes of each other, loving each other as much as they had that first moment they'd realized what they had.

I could feel Tempest in the cabin as I approached. The barriers she'd put up muted our bond, but she couldn't shut me out. No bonded could ever be completely cut off from each other. It was one of those things that was both good and bad. Good because it meant we were never truly alone, and bad for the exact same reason. Even though we weren't actually in each other's heads, it was close enough to be distracting.

As I stepped into the cabin, I felt my body automatically turning towards where I knew Tempest would be. It took a surprising amount of self-control not to look at her. Before today, I'd never been able to understand why bonded pairs seemed to literally gravitate towards each other. But gravity was a fairly accurate description. I'd felt a bit of a pull before we'd bonded, but now it was a nearly irresistible force.

Everyone's eyes turned towards me, and I knew it wasn't because they were waiting for me to give instructions on what to do. They wouldn't have stared at Tempest – well, maybe Annabella would've – but me, they could hide their curiosity behind my role as their leader. And I knew they were curious.

After all, I'd gone from being the only Qaniss who'd ever survived receiving the mark alone to being the oldest Qaniss to ever bond, and doing so after receiving my tattoo. Even though I was now bonded like them, I still wasn't like them.

I spoke as if nothing had changed. "Divide food and

medical supplies into packs for each of us. The rest we'll put into storage with extra clothes so we'll have things here when we come back. One change of clothes into each pack as well."

"What about weapons?" Annabella asked.

"Each take your own," I said. "Whatever you can carry into the spaces between. The rest, store here."

As they moved to do as I'd said, I felt eyes on me. They weren't Tempest's, that much I could tell. What I was getting from her now were waves of icy anger. I turned and found Tady watching me. I glared at her, but she didn't flinch. Instead, she raised her chin, two spots of color high on her cheeks.

"Bram," Emilia's voice drew my attention the other way.

I looked at her, grateful for the distraction. No matter how interested she was in what was happening with me, she'd never ask, especially not when we had more important things going on.

"Are you planning on us making caches of supplies on every world?" she asked. "Because we'll need to take stock of what money we have left."

I frowned. I hadn't thought of that. While the Qaniss weren't rich, we'd had an entire team of people who's job it had been to make sure we'd had currency for each world. They were gone too, along with everything they'd collected. All we had left was what we'd brought with us, and I knew it hadn't been very much, just the basic emergency packet every Qaniss group took with them.

"After we cross, we'll discuss the matter," I said. I managed not to sigh. I was a fighter, a warrior. This kind of planning had been one of the reasons I hadn't wanted to take over my dad's Council position.

"Maybe we could..." Emilia hesitated.

"What?" I prompted. We couldn't work without someone definitely in charge, but that didn't mean I wasn't open to ideas.

"We might want to consider trying to contact the *EV*," she suggested. "Or the Immortals."

That was actually a good idea. The Immortals only existed on one world, the result of a curse back during the time of the Tower of Babel. The *enverto venator*, however, were on more than one world, though what they hunted on each world varied. Some even went by different names. They all, however, knew of our existence, and often assisted us when the need arose. There was another group too, families who gathered information and passed it along to the *EV* or to the Immortals, though they fought no one.

I nodded. "I think that'd be good."

Harrison tapped Emilia on the shoulder, and the two began one of their private conversations, leaving me free to go back to sorting through my weapons to decide what I was going to take with me. In the end, I decided on all of them. I'd leave the new ones behind in case any of us ever needed them when we returned here.

Even my weapons, however, couldn't completely distract me from the negative emotions rolling across my bond with Tempest. When we were done here, I'd need to talk to her. Not working through it wasn't an option. We were bonded forever. It wasn't like we could simply walk away from each other.

By the time we'd all finished though, it was late, and we needed our rest if we were going to leave at first light. Traveling between the spaces of worlds required energy, especially since we had a long way to travel once we got there. As much as I hated what I was sensing from her, I knew the talk would have to wait.

Years of training would be the only reason I'd be able to fall asleep, and I was pretty sure Tempest wouldn't have the same luxury. All the more reason for me to sleep, I knew. I'd have to lend her my strength to travel.

The first time in the spaces between was always the most difficult. There wasn't any point in me telling her any of that though. I knew she wouldn't listen, especially not right now. The best I could do was to make it possible for me to have the energy to help her.

It didn't mean I had to like it.

****

I woke first, before the sun had risen, and for a moment I forgot where I was, forgot everything except the sheer terror that had pulled me from my sleep. It swept over me, nearly overwhelmed me, and I almost thought it was mine.

But it wasn't mine.

It was hers.

I stayed quiet as I grabbed the knife I always kept next to me. It had been a gift from my father on the day I'd received my tattoo. A six-inch double-sided blade, it was technically a dagger rather than something like a hunting knife. Usually best for close quarters combat rather than the sort of fighting I did with my swords, it was still made to kill.

And whatever was making Tempest feel that much terror was definitely going to die.

She'd chosen to sleep as far from me as possible, so I carefully made my way across the room, hoping not to wake the others. The last thing I needed was them to know something else was wrong. Annabella and Grady were on guard duty outside, and it was Fynn's turn to have the bed, so Kassia was on the floor in the small room with him, but there were enough of us that the floor in the main area of the cabin was still crowded, the myriad wings being used as blankets making it look like a rainbow of shimmering, glossy feathers.

In the far corner, Tempest was curled on her side, her wings tight against her back.

The only light we had came from the moon streaming in through the window, so Tempest's body was in the shadows, but I didn't need to see her to know she was in pain. She wasn't, however, awake. Whatever was scaring her badly enough to have woken me was happening inside her head.

I set my knife aside. It wouldn't do any good against a nightmare. A part of me knew it was most likely a bad idea, but I had to do it. I had to touch her, to offer strength and comfort to my bonded. It was a need so deeply engrained in my soul that I knew it had to come from Adonai.

The moment I put my hand on her shoulder, a shock ran through me. I couldn't move, couldn't speak...

I felt myself falling towards a whirlpool of darkness, tumbling past images and sounds that didn't make any sense. The cabin and the others were gone. It was only me in the darkness, me and the steadily growing fear.

Suddenly, I was on my feet, standing on something solid. I looked around, taking in the dirty concrete floor under my feet, the equally filthy concrete walls, the single watt bulb hanging from the ceiling. It offered barely enough light to see by, but barely was enough.

A tall post stood in the center of the room, and at the foot of the post was a body. Emaciated, so dirty it took me a moment to realize it was naked. Though its back was to me, I could see the glint of handcuffs around its wrists and metal cuffs around its ankles, both linked with chains to the post.

She. Not it. I knew the body was female. And I knew who it was without seeing her face. She tensed, and I heard the footsteps coming down the stairs.

I'd fallen into Tempest's nightmare.

Chapter Twenty-One

Tempest

I was shivering despite my resolution not to let him see me weak, but it was involuntary, out of my control after lying on the cold concrete for so long.

I didn't know how long I'd been down here. Hours. Years. There were no windows, no food to give me any indication of the passage of time. I had a small plastic bucket of water so I wouldn't dehydrate, and he knew how long he could starve me without anyone noticing. Not that I had anyone to notice. No one cared what happened to me. I'd known that all my life.

Footsteps sounded on the stairs and I tensed. He was coming back. He'd said he would, and no matter how much I wished he'd let me die down here, I knew that wasn't going to happen. I wouldn't get off so easily.

The first time he'd chained me down here, it had been for slapping his hand away when he'd put it on my knee. But that hadn't stopped me from refusing to cooperate the next time he'd done it. I'd take the punishments, but I'd never give in.

I pushed the thought aside. I didn't want to think about what he'd done the other times I'd been down here. I had the scars on my back to be reminders. Burn scars where he'd put his cigarettes out on me while he'd been...

My arms shook as I pushed myself into a sitting position, but I refused to take it lying down. Some people might've thought it was better to lay there and let him do what he wanted, to not provoke him. He was going to take what he wanted anyway. I couldn't fight him off. He was too much bigger than me, stronger. And he knew where to hit so no one ever saw the marks so long as I wore the clothes he gave me.

Still, I fought however I could.

I'd tried to run away, and that was why I was in my current state. The police had caught me, and brought me back. I didn't try to tell them why I'd run. They were his friends. They'd never believe me. He had too many friends in too many places for me to be able to trust anyone.

I didn't listen when he started to speak. It was the same every time. Asking me why I'd committed whatever particular sin had gotten me here in the first place, why I was forcing him to hurt me. How he didn't want to treat me this way, but I'd given him no choice.

The scent of his cigarettes made me want to gag, but I didn't make a sound. That always made him more angry, but I refused to give him the satisfaction of a response. I waited to hear what the punishment would be this time. Sometimes he used his belt, sometimes a switch from one of the trees outside.

This time, however, I heard a different sound. A loud crack made me jump with surprise. He laughed, and I knew he thought I'd moved because I was afraid.

I didn't look back at him, but he walked around in front of me. I kept my eyes looking straight ahead and tried not to think about the pain in my knees or the way my muscles were trembling with fatigue.

"I bought something for you." His voice was oddly high-pitched for his size, and I'd wanted to laugh the first time I'd heard it. I'd quickly learned it had been a good thing I hadn't.

Something dropped into my line of sight and my stomach rebelled as I realized what it was.

A whip.

An honest-to-goodness leather whip.

For a moment, I thought I wasn't going to be able to control myself, and would throw up what little water I'd consumed while I'd been down here. I didn't have anything else to come up, which was probably the only reason I managed not to gag.

He walked back around behind me and I closed my eyes, waiting.

The first blow made me gasp; the second made me sway. They were sharp bursts of pain spreading out in heat across the rest of my skin. I managed to stay upright through at least half a dozen and then my exhausted body couldn't manage it anymore. I dropped to the floor, dimly surprised to feel the hot wet of blood against my skin. I hadn't even realized my back was bleeding.

The world began to gray as he kept hitting me ,and my last thought before I slipped into unconsciousness was that, at least this time, I wouldn't be awake when he started to rape me...

****

I jerked awake, shoving at the hand on me. My heart was racing, lungs burning as I dragged in air. I didn't know where I was, who was touching me.

"Tempest."

My wings were flared, out in a defensive position. I scrambled up so my back was against the wall, my hand automatically going to my knife. I'd pulled it out before I truly registered the voice that had said my name.

Bram.

He crouched in front of me, his hands up and open, palms out so I could see he had no weapon. His face was white, and the realization hit me almost like a physical blow.

"What..." My voice shook. "Were you in my head?"

"I didn't know," he said. "I didn't know that could happen."

I was going to throw up. "You saw..."

I didn't need him to answer. The horror on his face said it

all. I stood up.

"Stay away from me."

I pushed past him, stepping over whichever of the twins was sleeping on the floor, and then I was at the door. He didn't call after me, and that was good because I didn't want to have this conversation, and certainly not with all of the others listening in.

Annabella and Grady were outside the cabin, and while both gave me strange looks when I practically ran by, neither said anything. Tady's words came back to me about how when two people were bonded, they were each other's responsibility, and I knew, if anyone was going to come after me, it'd be Bram.

I began to jog, heading towards the path he'd taken me on before. Before I could figure out what I wanted to do about Bram, I had to shake off the nightmare. I didn't dream about that night very often, but when I did, it was always hard to move past it when I woke.

My back ached even though I knew it was just the memory of pain. He'd almost killed me that night, and I still didn't remember what had stopped him. I only knew I'd woken up in the hospital, and once I'd recovered, I'd been put in a new group home. I'd asked what had happened, but no one had told me. I'd considered doing some snooping on my own, but had ultimately decided I preferred not to have to think about it. The scars were memory enough.

I let the run clear my head, or at least I attempted to. It was impossible to forget Bram had seen everything. Well, not all of the horrors in my past, but that one had been enough. I didn't want him to know anymore. I didn't want anyone to know.

I hated that look of pity I got. It was worse than the people who were disgusted, as if I'd somehow asked for what had happened to me.

I could feel Bram wanting me to come back, to talk to him, but he didn't seem to be pursuing me, so I let it go. I didn't want to see him. Ever.

I wished I'd never let him talk me into this stupid bonding. I wished I'd never come to Fort Prince in the first place. Never met the Qaniss, and found out what I was. I would've been happy being on my own, never having to worry about anyone else. Now, no matter how angry I was at Bram, I knew I couldn't let him leave without me. It would tear me apart. I could feel it, the way he was connected to me.

I hated it.

And I hated knowing he loved me even more.

I didn't want any of it.

I stayed away until the sun started to rise, and I knew it was almost time for us to go. I'd made a decision while I was running and I intended to stick with it, no matter what happened. I would travel with the rest of the group to the other world. I'd stay with them, but I wouldn't be one of them.

And I was going to close off the bond between Bram and I.

I never wanted to feel this connection again. I'd learned young to not let people close, and I'd been foolish enough to think this time it'd be different because it was supposed to be some sort of supernatural thing.

I could shut it down, I knew, and while I might not be able to completely leave the group, I'd at least be able to protect myself.

I wouldn't forget again.

Chapter Twenty-Two

Bram

Tempest leaving the cabin woke the others, but I didn't do anything more than assure them we weren't under attack. I couldn't tell them I'd gone into her nightmare. I hadn't known that was even possible. Bonded pairs could speak telepathically, but it was essentially like talking verbally, not mind-reading. We had to form the words consciously. We could sense each other's feelings, but I'd never heard of any bonded being able to get into each other's heads like that.

I could only imagine how violated Tempest had to feel, and she had every right to feel that way. My only defense was that I hadn't done it intentionally. All I'd wanted to do was wake her, take her out of her nightmare. Instead, I'd damaged the fragile relationship we'd been working towards. I wanted to go after her and apologize, tell her I hadn't meant to see any of it.

I knew that wouldn't work though. She didn't want me to come after her. I could feel her anger – no, that word wasn't strong enough. Fury. That was what she was feeling right now. I didn't know if she understood it had been an accident, but I didn't think it mattered. I'd seen something private. Something horrible.

I felt sick as I stepped outside. The air was crisp, cold, but even that didn't make me feel any better. It wasn't only the gut-wrenching pain of betrayal I felt coming from Tempest, but also the utter revulsion at what I'd seen.

Lucan had said he'd seen scars on her back that had appeared to be evidence of prior abuse. I hadn't seen the scars, other than a few hints of them across her shoulders, but now I'd watched her receive them.

I walked around the back of the cabin to avoid being seen, and promptly threw up. I'd borne my fair share of pain, both physical and emotional. Nothing, however, had prepared me for watching, helplessly, as the woman I loved had been brutally abused.

My hands curled into fists and I closed my eyes, willing myself to calm down. I could feel my wings pulsing against my back. Tempest had enough of her own emotions to deal with. She didn't need to feel mine as well. I was her bonded, and I loved her. It was my responsibility to protect her, to support her.

When I finally felt like I could walk without throwing up or screaming, I opened my eyes, and headed down to the river to rinse my mouth. We had water in the cabin, but I wasn't composed enough to go back yet.

Even as I knelt next to the river, I kept seeing the

nightmare. Unable to do anything as the man taunted her. Whipped her until her back bled. Started to undress. I hadn't needed much imagination to know what had happened next.

My stomach heaved again, and I spit out the water onto the grass before I gagged.

I'd known about the physical abuse based on the scars. I'd suspected the possibility that she'd been sexually abused as well. But knowing and suspecting were completely different than seeing.

"Adonai..."

Words failed me as I pushed myself to my feet. I could barely think, much less pray. How was I supposed to pray about something like this? I'd seen horrible things, done horrible things, but they had always been done by demons or to demons.

I wasn't an idiot. I knew humans could do things just as awful. I'd never seen it happen right in front of me before. If I had, I might not have been able to refrain from doing to them what I did to demons. I'd known of Qaniss who had killed humans, but until I'd gone into Tempest's nightmare, I'd never known the urge to do it myself.

"Adonai." I tried again.

My chest hurt. I'd lost everything, and then I'd found her. I'd never believed I would bond with anyone, that I would even fall in love like a normal person. Not only had I found my bonded, but I'd formed a love bond with her too. I went from being alone to being more closely connected to a person than I'd ever thought possible. And now, this.

"Adonai." I went to my knees and buried my face in my hands. My wings wrapped around me. "Please, Father."

I waited for an answer, but none came. What did come was dawn, and with it, the knowledge that it was time to go. And time to face Tempest again.

I stood, my joints popping as I went. I had to think, but I didn't have the luxury right now. The trip from Fort Prince to Wycliffe would take some time. It'd be better to wait until then.

It took a bit more effort than usual, but I managed to clear my mind as I walked back around the cabin. The others were already there and I could see the concern on a couple faces. The fact that Tempest was standing at the fringe of the group with only her things told me this was going to be even harder than I thought.

Without a word, I went into the cabin, gathered my things, and went back out. I trusted the others had all done their jobs, and we were ready to go. Despite the negative emotions I could feel radiating off of Tempest, I walked over to her.

"Bonded pairs are the only ones who can travel between

worlds," I said. I kept my voice even and without emotion. "We have to channel our power together."

"How do we know where we're going?" she asked.

Her own voice was flat, and I didn't for a moment think that meant she was okay.

"It's a bit complicated to explain," I said. "You have to feel it."

She glared at me.

"I'm not trying to be difficult." I softened my tone. "Qaniss spend years learning how to do this, and we don't have that kind of time. I'll focus for us on this trip. It means I'll need you to channel more of your energy."

"I don't know how." She scowled.

I stretched out my wings, and heard the others doing the same. Our power may have fueled the travel, but we used our wings to move. She did the same, and I had a moment to appreciate the strength and elegance I saw there. Then I held out my hand. I knew she didn't want to touch me, but I needed her to. For this to work, we had to be touching. Her face was blank, but she put her hand in mine. I ignored the warmth flooding through me when our hands touched.

I looked at the others, and they were ready. I glanced at Tempest. She wasn't looking at me, but I could feel the energy coursing through our hands. At least power wasn't going to be an issue. She mimicked me as I curled my wings around us so we were cocooned in a tight circle.

I took a deep breath and closed my eyes. Usually, this was simple for me, but I'd never done this with someone else before. It was still easy for me to find the crack, the place where I could reach outside the world, and pull myself out of this world and into the spaces between.

Pulling power through Tempest, I twisted us both, and felt the familiar squeezing sensation as we went.

Immediately, I felt the difference, traveling with her. I'd always found the between spaces to be cold and dark, places where I'd always felt more alone than anyplace else. This time though, I didn't feel alone. I wasn't alone. I could feel her. As reluctant as she was, she was here.

And suddenly, we were there. Stepping out of the space, and onto a mountain on another world.

Automatically, the others drew their weapons, and spread out in the usual formation to check the area. While we'd been told the fight would be in Wycliffe, demons weren't exactly known for their honesty, even when being tortured. It just as easily could've been setting us up for an ambush.

A quick look around said we were alone. There was no cabin on this mountain, telling me this was a world different enough from the last that whoever had built the cabin we'd been staying at hadn't done it here. I wasn't concerned about the why though. We needed to do what we'd been sent to do.

Stop the demons in Wycliffe.

"Leigh and Lucan, take first watch. We'll go in hour shifts." I slid my knife back into the sheath at my waist.

"Shouldn't we be looking for a vehicle to get us to Wycliffe?" Annabella asked.

I shook my head. "We can't waste time on trying to find a car, and plotting a route to Ohio. If we're lucky, we can make it in a day and half driving straight through. We'd then have to scout the location and fight."

"You want us to travel there," Lucan said.

"I thought we couldn't travel to a different place, just a different world." Tempest looked at Tady when she spoke, not me.

Tady glanced at me, and I gave her a sharp nod. This wasn't the time to push Tempest.

"It takes more power to travel within a world, ya ken?" Tady said. "Once we get to a world, it is possible to travel to a different place, but not a good idea if yer plannin' on fightin' right away."

"We'll stay here for a few hours," I addressed the entire group. "Gather our energy. Then we'll travel to Wycliffe, and use the night to recover and scout the location, with plans to attack in the morning."

"Are you sure that's wise?" Annabella asked. "Shouldn't we conserve our energy, and travel in a more conventional way?"

"The demons said Wycliffe was being attacked. It may feel like we're wasting time, but it's actually the fastest way there." I kept my tone firm. Like my fellow Qaniss, I hated the idea of sitting still, but I knew it was for the best. I looked at Tempest. "And you need to know what to expect when we get there."

"I'm fine," she snapped.

The others didn't need to have a bond to know she was pissed at me.

"No," I said. "You're not. You need to know how to fight the different kinds of demons. The best ways to kill, or at least incapacitate them."

As I spoke to Tempest, the others scattered, pairs moving about to where they could spar. It wasn't our physical energy we needed to conserve. Staying loose was a good thing.

"Pick the weapon you want to fight with," I said. "I'll tell you what you need to know."

I knew she was mad, but I didn't think she'd be willing to go into a fight without preparing herself. Five minutes into the sparring match, I knew that wasn't the case.

She fought angry, coming after me with her little

switchblade, not listening to a word I said about where to aim, about the differences between killing a *spinis* versus an *excoriator*.

I grabbed her wrist as she made yet another feeble attempt to stab me. A quick twist of my hand, and her knife fell to the ground again. She shoved me away, eyes flashing.

She was never going to learn this way.

I sighed and shook my head. "Look, I know you're mad at me."

"I don't want to talk about it," she cut me off.

I kept going anyway. "It was an accident. I didn't know that could happen, but that's not what I want to talk to you about. You need to let me teach you."

"I'm not interested in anything you have to offer," she sneered at me, giving me a thoroughly contemptuous look before walking away.

I ran my hand through my hair. That had gone well.

I'd spent the first couple years after receiving my tattoo wishing I had a bonded. Someone to have my back, someone who'd understand me, and not simply say they did. I'd come to accept being alone, but when I'd first seen Tempest and had realized who she was, I'd found myself believing I would finally have someone. I'd seen how close the others were and believed that's what I had to look forward to.

"Instead, I get her," I muttered as I watched her walk away. "Thanks."

If you could choose, would you want someone else?

The question startled me, as much because I hadn't been expecting an answer as for what He asked.

Would I want someone else? I hadn't even considered it. I'd felt her presence almost from the beginning, and even when I'd been trying to deny it, there'd been no doubt in my mind we belonged together. I'd never thought about what I'd do if I'd had a choice in the matter.

Tempest was head-strong, and probably one of the most stubborn people I'd ever met, and that was saying something. She clearly had serious baggage in her past, things that kept her from trusting people, and trust was one of the most important things between bonded. She held grudges, fought without thinking, had a temper. Despite all that had happened to her, she felt things passionately. She was too independent, thinking she never needed to rely on anyone else.

That part at least, I forced myself to admit, was exactly like me.

Which was why we shouldn't work together. Why, out of all of the Qaniss, she never should have been chosen for me and I for her. We were supposed to complement each other. Strengthen each other's weaknesses. We weren't supposed to have the same weaknesses.

Then again, the rational part of my brain spoke up, I'd been so used to doing things on my own, would I really want a partner who went along with whatever I said? Did I need someone to agree with me, or someone strong enough to stand up to me? Beyond needing it, did I *want* that? Did I want to have a bonded who wasn't strong, who didn't know her own mind?

I scowled as I admitted the answer. No. I didn't want it, and it wasn't what I needed. I needed someone like Tempest to face off against me, to push me. I wanted that, even if it meant moments like this. And I didn't just want someone like her.

I wanted her.

The more I got to know her, the more I fell in love with her. I'd seen only a fraction of what she'd suffered, and the fact that she hadn't completely broken spoke of how strong she truly was. But her strength was only one of the many reasons I was drawn to her, and I knew my love would only grow the more I knew her.

If she'd let me get to know her. I had to figure out how to get through to her.

Any suggestions?

Silence.

Of course not. That would be too easy.

I looked around at the others. They were all busy practicing, staying warmed up in case we ran into any demons when we traveled again later. It was clear Tempest didn't want to have anything to do with me at the moment, and it wasn't the best time or place to force the issue. Once we got to Wycliffe, after we'd secured things, and were bunking down for the night, I'd make sure she and I got first watch so we could talk, work things out.

With my plan firmly in mind, I decided to go for a jog.

I hadn't taken into consideration the possibility that Adonai might've had other plans.

By the time I called everyone to the clearing a few hours later, I could feel that some of the anger from Tempest had dissipated. That was good. She stepped up next to me without me having to ask her, and that was even better.

"I want to do it this time."

I looked down at her in surprise as her wings unfurled. She didn't meet my eyes, but at least she was there and talking to me.

"I can visualize Wycliffe," she continued. "I know it's not the same as the one where I grew up, but I know it. It's the best time for me to practice."

I couldn't argue with her logic on that even if I hadn't already been inclined to let her do it, if only to ease things between us. Bonded fought with each other, but even at their worst, I'd never heard of one trying to pull away, and I knew that's what she wanted to do.

I held out my hand, and she took it as we wrapped our wings around us. I closed my eyes, and tried to clear my mind. I'd never had someone else lead before, and it was harder than I'd realized to keep my own thoughts from interfering. Finally, I focused on her hand, and thought only about channeling power into her as I felt her reaching towards the space between.

There was a sharp twist, a jerk and then we were between.

My fingers tightened around hers, and she pulled more energy from me.

Another jerk and we were standing in a field.

I watched the others pop into existence around us. Traveling as a group meant one pair went first, and the others focused on them to guide the exact position. I supposed that would be a lesson for another day.

Tempest yanked her hand out of mine even as I was opening my mouth to tell her she'd done well. Before I could get a word out, I felt her slam down a wall across our bond.

I winced at the sharp pain that went through me, my hand automatically going to my chest. What had she done? I couldn't feel her, couldn't sense her. I knew we were still bonded because we were both alive, but she'd managed to do something I'd never thought possible.

She'd closed off our bond.

"Tempest." I took a step towards her. "What did..."

"Leave me alone, Bram." Her voice was cold. "I'm here because I have to be. I have enough self-preservation for that, but I'm going to do whatever it takes to free myself from you. I don't want to have anything to do with any of this. Or with you."

I stared at her for a moment. A thousand retorts sprang to mind. Why had she even bothered to bond in the first place? Why hadn't she just stayed on her world? Every one of her words cut me, adding to the empty pain of our closed bond.

"Fine." I heard the word before I'd realized I was going to say it. "I'd been doing great on my own."

"I'll go find somewhere else to sleep." She started to walk away.

"Don't bother." The words were ice in my mouth. "I'll leave."

I didn't wait to see if she'd protest. She wouldn't, I already knew. She didn't care about me, or about anyone, or anything. She was only looking out for herself. She could never be a Qaniss, no matter whose blood ran in her veins.

It came as no surprise to me that Adonai stayed silent as I

stomped off. He was always silent when I needed Him.

Chapter Twenty-Three

Tempest

I'd been completely prepared to storm away while Bram watched. I'd almost been looking forward to being able to do that to him. I may have been calm on the outside, but I'd been seething from the moment I'd woken from my nightmare and realized Bram had seen it all. I'd been furious, humiliated, and the fact that it was clear he hadn't done it on purpose actually made it worse. I could handle cruelty, could handle someone being malicious, but what I didn't want was someone pitying me.

I hadn't been prepared for what had actually happened though. Hearing him say he'd been fine on his own had hurt more than I'd expected, and more than I wanted it to. I wanted to feel relief that he wasn't going to fight me, that he'd been the one to walk away. Instead, I felt a pain that had nothing to do with the bond I was currently keeping closed, and had everything to do with the hurt I could see on his face.

I tightened my hold on the bond. I had no idea how I was doing it, but in my head, I envisioned it like kinking a garden hose to stem off the water. However I did it, I wanted it to continue. I wasn't really sure that I meant what I'd said about not wanting anything to do with the Qaniss anymore, but I did know I didn't want to be near him, not after he'd seen...

It wasn't until after Bram had disappeared from view that I realized everyone else was staring at me. I didn't look at anyone in particular as I scowled. Aside from Tady, I didn't really have an opinion about anyone.

Well, that wasn't entirely accurate. Lucan was nice enough, and I wasn't fond of Annabella. The rest I were pretty much just there as far as I was concerned.

"Leigh, Lucan, patrol out five hundred yards. Make sure we don't have anyone nearby, human or otherwise." Annabella's voice was clear and firm as she gave out orders.

I waited for her to tell me what to do, if only so I could let loose some of the anger inside, but she didn't. She ignored me. If I'd needed a sign to tell me I didn't belong, Annabella's clear dismissal of my presence was good enough for me.

I went off in the direction opposite as Bram had gone. I didn't want to risk running into him. Not after that. I didn't have any specific place in mind, only the overwhelming need to be alone.

I'd always been a loner, even the few times I'd been in good situations. My latest shrink had implied more than once that perhaps I suffered from some form of social anxiety disorder or maybe even autism, and that was why I didn't relate well to people. She also agreed with previous psychiatric diagnosis that I was narcissistic, so she'd also speculated I didn't like being around people because I thought I was better and smarter than everyone else.

That wasn't entirely true. I knew I was smarter than most people, but I didn't think I was better than anyone.

I was halfway through the outskirts of town when I realized I'd been heading into Wycliffe. I was pretty sure the others wouldn't have let me go if they'd known where I'd end up, but that was all the more reason for me to want to keep walking. It wasn't my Wycliffe, and I still didn't know all the rules about how this whole parallel world thing worked, but I still knew this place. And, for once, familiar was a good thing.

I shivered as a gust of wind cut across the street, sending dried leaves dancing in front of my feet. It was almost dark, and I could hear parents calling their kids in form after-school play.

I glanced up at a street sign and realized with a start where I was. This had been the part of Wycliffe where the well-to-do families had always lived, the ones who weren't exactly rich but were a bit more than middle-class. It looked pretty much the same, or at least how I'd always imagined it to be. None of my foster families or group homes had been there.

I frowned suddenly, stopping in the middle of the sidewalk. Something wasn't right. The air felt colder, but I couldn't figure out how it would've dropped so much between one step and the last. Maybe it was a scent, something rotten on the wind, but when I tried taking a deep breath, I couldn't smell anything.

I couldn't explain it, but it almost felt like it had in the shed back on the other world, back when Bram had tortured the demon. Like something cold and slimy had slithered across my skin. Like I was lost in the dark, some place that I could never get out of. It was all of these things and none of them.

Demons.

They were close by, here in this nice neighborhood.

I knew I should go back and get the others. They needed to know, and they were the only ones who could stop them. Despite my insistence to Bram that I didn't need to train, I knew I couldn't handle what those things were. Definitely not alone. The smart thing would've been to go back and talk to Tady, have her tell the others.

I may have been a genius, but that didn't always mean I did the smart thing.

This was going to be one of those times I did something dumb.

I closed my eyes, and let myself feel for the disturbance, for the evil, for whatever it was that spoke between a Qaniss and a demons. I found it, and started to walk. With every step,

I told myself this was stupid, but I still didn't go back. For reasons I didn't quite understand, I kept putting one foot in front of the other.

After a few minutes, I found myself in front of an iron gate. The wall around the property was brick and at least ten feet high. I didn't know who lived here, but whoever it was had...guests. I couldn't say for sure how I knew this was the place, but I did.

I looked around to make sure no one was watching and stretched my wings out. I'd never flown before, not really, only moved between the spaces, but my only other option was to go back and get the others. I almost changed my mind, but then I heard it. Faint, but recognizable.

The sound of flesh hitting flesh.

A grunt of pain.

A man's grunt.

I supposed it could've been someone fighting in self-defense, but instinct told me that wasn't the case. The demons had a person in there and they were hurting him.

I pushed off with my feet, and flapped my wings...and almost flew straight into the gate. I grabbed the top of it, and flipped myself over. It was easier to use the wings to slow my fall, and I managed to land on my feet without stumbling. Before I went any further, I pulled out my knife. Bram didn't think I could do any damage with the switchblade, but it was better than my bare hands.

The property was large, but I didn't need to search. I knew where to go. It wasn't until I was a few feet away from the back door that it hit me.

The smell of the demons. The strange hissing and crackling sound I knew was language. The thud of someone being hit.

All of that faded away when I felt it.

Even through the walls I'd put up, I felt it...felt *him.*

Bram.

They had Bram.

I was going to kill them all.

Chapter Twenty-Four

Bram

I was still trying to figure out where things had gone wrong.

After I'd left Tempest and the others, I'd kept walking. I'd been seething, furious at her for closing off the bond, for taking away something I hadn't realized I'd wanted, I'd needed. I'd hated her, but I'd still loved her too.

My thoughts had been chaotic, so much so I hadn't seen or felt them coming.

It takes a lot to knock a Qaniss unconscious, but they managed it. When I came to, I was in what looked like a basement, chains around my wrists and ankles. Three *ardens lingua* stood in front of me, and I could see a couple *excoriator* on one side, a *spinis* on the other. At least six demons, and I had no weapons, no limbs free. And with Tempest closed off from me, I had no way of getting any help.

"Wings," one of the *ardens lingua* hissed, jabbing a bony finger at me. "Want to see your wings."

"Not going to happen." I pushed myself up on my knees, tugging at the chains as I moved. They were locked down tight. Either the demons had been here for a while, or the human who owned the house had some seriously questionable hobbies.

"Wings!"

I shook my head. They weren't going to kill me quickly. If they'd wanted me dead, it would've happened on the path in the woods where they'd found me. The fact I was still breathing meant they wanted to torture me first. Torture me for information, maybe. Most likely, they wanted to torture me for the fun of it. Their fun, obviously, because it definitely wasn't going to be mine.

The *ardens lingua took turns punching me to get warmed up.* A couple to my face but most to my torso. I didn't even have enough give with the chains to pull my arms in to protect my ribs and stomach. I stopped counting the cracks I heard after the fourth one. I didn't want to know.

"Put out your wings and we stop."

I wasn't sure which one said it. They all pretty much sounded the same, and if they were the same species, they looked it too. It didn't matter which one said it though. I knew what they wanted. I'd seen the broken and twisted bodies of Qaniss who had been tortured before. Seen how their wings had been torn off. I may not have had much room to fight, but I was going to make it as hard as possible for them to break me.

I spit out some blood, and grinned up at them. "Don't tell

me you're getting tired already."

Less than ten minutes later, blood was streaming down my jaw and neck from two cuts, and my shirt was a total loss. Between the *spinis* and the *excoriators*, I had more than two dozen holes dotting my chest and back, each one oozing blood and sending pain screaming across my nerves.

And they were just getting started.

Things were going to get a lot worse, I knew. They would peel the skin and flesh from my body. Break my bones. I wouldn't betray the others, but that was about all I could know for sure. Anything else...I might give in.

As I steeled myself for whatever was coming next, things went from bad to worse.

I heard the back door slam open seconds before I felt her.

My heart leaped into my throat and I stared at the demons, willing them to not have heard it. When they turned towards the basement stairs, I knew there was only one thing I could do.

"Run, Tempest!" I screamed the words as loudly as I could. If she could close off the bond, she might be able to survive my death. It was her only chance.

Adonai, save her!

The footsteps told me she hadn't listened. That wasn't really a surprise. She never listened.

She wasn't running, either away or towards. She was walking. Walking slowly and deliberately down the stairs. When she stepped into view, my heart thudded against my chest. Her wings were spread, her eyes burning. In one hand, she held her little switchblade. In the other, she had one of my swords. The demons must've left it upstairs.

"You need to back off."

Her voice was filled with a quiet kind of fury and the hair on the back of my neck prickled. She pointed the sword at me.

"No one touches him. He's mine."

I suddenly couldn't feel anything. She said I was hers.

Her eyes narrowed. "If anyone gets to kill him, it's me."

Okay, so her claiming me didn't sound so great anymore, but I wasn't really in a place to argue.

"Run, Tempest." I tried to make it a command, but it came out like the plea it was. "Please."

She ignored me.

Again.

The demons were staring at her. They'd seen Qaniss before, so it wasn't like a person with wings was freaking them out. I wasn't sure if it was the fact that she had a switchblade, or something else, but whatever it was, it gave her the chance to lunge at them before they decided to end things quickly.

She attacked silently, swinging my sword with her left

hand even as she stabbed with her right. The closest *excoriator* watched its arm drop to the floor, and then lurched sideways as Tempest stabbed the side of its neck with her switchblade. I saw a surge of power go through the weapon, but it wasn't enough to kill the demon. Still, it stumbled back, knocking one of its counterparts backwards.

I pulled against the chains, ignoring the new flood of pain each movement sent through my body. They were going to kill her. She was amazing, twirling and swinging with surprising accuracy considering she was using her left hand and a sword she'd never practiced with, but being amazing wasn't going to be good enough. She'd taken them by surprise, but she didn't have the power to kill them, not alone. Not like this. She didn't know how to channel it correctly.

"Open the bond!" I finally yelled it at her as one of the *excoriator* claws barely missed her arm. "Please, Tempest!"

I didn't care that I was angry at her or she was angry at me. It didn't matter. I needed her to survive because losing her would kill me. I knew it as surely as I knew Adonai had chosen her for me. I might've been able to survive having Adonai's power alone again, but I couldn't live without her.

She glared at me and, for a moment, I thought she wouldn't do it. Blood streamed from a cut across her forehead, and the side of her face was already swelling. She was holding her own, but she was starting to tire. I could feel it as the bond wavered. She was using too much of her energy trying to keep me out.

As the *spinis* dove for her feet, she tried to spin out of the way and stumbled.

I saw it all happening in slow motion.

An *ardens lingua* swung, and made contact with her shoulder. She let out a grunt as her shoulder popped out of place, the sword falling to the floor.

I didn't know if it was the pain, or if she did it voluntarily, but suddenly, the bond opened. I gritted my teeth at the sudden rush of power and pain. I needed to help her. Now.

I wrapped my fingers around the chains holding my arms in place. I didn't know if this would work, but Tempest was trying to stab the *spinis* with her switchblade using her only working arm. She didn't have much time.

Adonai, help me.

I sent a rush of energy through the chains and then pulled. My muscles strained, screaming, and then, suddenly, the bolts came free. I yelled as I swung the chain towards the *spinis*, flooding the metal with so much power that the demon exploded the moment the end of the chain hit it.

Tempest's head snapped up, and a sharp stab of pain went through me as she turned and slammed her shoulder into a post, pushing her shoulder joint back into place. A flood of relief was followed by a rush of endorphins and adrenaline that coursed through both of us.

My feet were still chained, but the ones connected to my arms had more than enough reach. I snapped out the chains as Tempest grabbed my sword again.

I felt her question even as she shoved the sword through the back of an *excoriator*. I didn't try to explain it. I couldn't have even if I'd wanted to. It wasn't the kind of thing that could really be explained. Instead, I reached across the bond, into her, and pushed the power into the sword.

For a moment, she fought against me, and then, with an almost audible sigh, she let go. I felt her reach back across the bond to me, and everything suddenly clicked.

We moved together, her driving the demons back towards me while I used the only weapons I had. One chain wrapped around the neck of an *excoriator*, and I pulled with enough force to rip its head off. She slammed her switchblade into the eye of an *ardens lingua*, and jumped back to avoid its blood as it gushed out. We fought without a word, with barely a sound, and then, suddenly, it was over, and we were surrounded by bodies.

She turned to look at me and, as our eyes met, I knew she wasn't going to close off the bond. I nodded and she returned it. We might still need to talk, but we were good again.

Then my knees buckled, and I fell to the concrete floor, sending a new shock of pain through me. She was hazy as she came towards me, and it was all I could do to fight back the darkness that wanted me. It would've been nice to give in, but we weren't safe here. We had to get back to the others, and we both needed to heal.

These demons weren't the only ones in Wycliffe, and it was going to take all of us, together, to save the city.

Chapter Twenty-Five

Tempest

For a minute, I thought he was going to fall, and that would've been bad. I could feel the adrenaline leaving my body, and knew there was no way I'd be able to carry him back to the others. At the moment, I wasn't even sure I could manage to get back there myself.

I stumbled towards him, and then frowned as I realized his ankles were still chained. I looked back at the bodies and my stomach churned at the thought of having to try to figure out where they'd put the keys. I knelt next to Bram, my hand automatically going out to touch him. I pulled back right before I made contact, torn between needing to make sure he was okay, and remembering what had happened every other time I'd touched him, the flare of power...the hint of something else.

"Go." His voice was more firm than I'd thought it could be. "Get the others."

"I'm not leaving you here." It wasn't even a question. I'd known the moment I'd realized the demons had him. Not being with him was no longer an option. I still had issues with this entire situation, but I knew now more than ever that leaving wasn't something I could even consider.

"You have to," he said. His eyes met mine and I could see the pain he was trying to hide. "There's no key."

I gave him a puzzled look, then followed his gaze as he looked at the manacles around his ankles. No keyholes. I reached out and took his left hand. I heard him suck in a breath at the spark of energy that came as soon as we touched, but neither of us said anything. The manacle around his wrist didn't have a keyhole either. It looked liked they'd been fused together once they'd been put on him.

"How were they going to let you out?" I asked, unaware I'd asked it out loud until he answered.

"Cut off my feet and hands, and the chains will slip right off." His voice was matter-of-fact.

My head jerked up, and he shrugged, wincing at the movement. I felt his pain wash over me.

"Tempest..."

"Quiet." I released his hand, and went back to the chains on the floor. "I need to figure out how to get these off of you." I gave him a quick glance as I added, "Without having to cut off your feet."

That got me a ghost of a smile, but even if I hadn't been able to feel his pain across the bond, I would've see it in his face, his eyes.

God, what do I do? For the first time in a long time, I said it as a prayer and not a curse. *I know You're real. Even when I was trying to pretend you weren't, I knew You existed. It's always been about whether or not You cared. If You care about Bram – not even me, but him – help us. He's dedicated everything to You, and this is what it's gotten Him. If You've truly called us to this mission or whatever it is, I need to get him out of here, because I'm not leaving here alone, no matter what it means for me.*

I gasped as I felt heat and power rush through me, and into the chain around Bram's ankle. He said my name, but I didn't acknowledge it, too busy staring at the metal fracturing under my hands. As soon as it broke and fell away, I touched Bram's ankle, sure the skin had to have been burnt, but it was smooth, not even raw from the manacle.

I turned to the other one. I felt Bram's eyes on me as the second chain fell to the floor. My hands went to his left wrist, then his right. I made sure I didn't touch his tattoo, unsure what would happen with all this energy pulsing through me, but I didn't shake off his hand when he touched my forearm.

"Thank you."

I nodded and stood, holding out my hand. He took it, and I felt his pain flicker into me. He fought it back, but I wasn't going to let him do that. Not when I could take some of it. I wasn't sure how to do it, but I acted on instinct, pulling his pain into my body. I gritted my teeth, but the look of surprise and relief on his face was worth it.

"Tempest." He tugged his hand away, his wings snapping out to compensate for the loss of support. "That's enough. You can't take it all. We both have to get back to the others."

I nodded, not trusting myself to speak. If this was only a fraction of what he was feeling, I was suddenly worried about the extent of his injuries. This wasn't the time for it though. I needed to get him back to Lucan to be healed. I wasn't sure how much I'd be able to help this time. My shoulder was throbbing with a deep ache, and I knew it needed some healing of its own if I was going to be able to use it in the upcoming fight.

I pulled his arm around my shoulders, and used my wings to help keep Bram steady as we started for the stairs.

It took us nearly an hour to get back to the others, and by the time we reached Kassia and Fynn who'd been posted as sentries, both Bram and I were about ready to drop. How we made it those last few feet without needing help, I didn't know.

Yes, I did. I knew Who had given us the strength to make it back. Who'd given me the power to break Bram's chains. And I knew as soon as we'd finished telling the others what had happened, and having our wounds tended to, I was going to need to face it. Face Him.

I'd fully expected the others to be looking for us, concerned that we weren't around. More than that, I'd expected them to freak out when they saw me half-carrying Bram, both of us covered in our own blood as well as the black ichor of demon blood. I knew we healed faster than non-Qaniss, but it wasn't instant, especially not from the amount of injuries we'd sustained.

None of them even blinked an eye or asked what happened. Despite the fact that Bram was more injured than I was, he filled the others in on what had happened while Lucan patched us up. What Bram didn't mention was anything about our bond, my nightmare, or what I'd done to the chains even though I hadn't asked him to keep any of it a secret. I appreciated it though. This whole bond thing was still so new to me and having to deal with the others' opinions about Bram seeing my dream or me closing off the bond wasn't something I wanted to deal with at the moment. We had more immediate things to think about. Like healing.

Any places where Bram and I were both bleeding had already stopped on their own so all Lucan could do was make sure the wounds were clean. Bram's were deeper than the cut on my forehead, and if we'd been normal people, he'd have gone to the hospital for stitches. As it was, Lucan simply bandaged things as best he could, gave us both a bit of the creation power he used to prompt healing, and tied my arm up. All we could do then was try to sleep and hope we healed enough overnight that we'd be able to fight the next day.

Because of our injuries, Bram and I were excused from guard duty since we had more than enough pairs to cover the rest of the night. Instead of finding a place as far as possible from Bram like I had the night before, I stayed close.

He didn't speak as he stretched out on the ground next to the fire the others had built while we'd been gone, weariness radiating from his body. I hoped the heat from the fire would help our aching muscles enough that we'd be able to sleep.

I'd asked him about the fire, wanting to know if it was a good idea to have one going when we knew there were demons around. He'd told me Adonai had given Annabella a protective quality to her power, and she could shield us for a few hours overnight. I didn't even bother to ask how that worked. I'd already figured out that ninety percent of the time, when it came to something with Adonai's power, the answer was generally some version of 'I can't explain it exactly.'

I could feel Bram's exhaustion as he folded his arms under his head and closed his eyes. I was tired too, but my mind was too busy to let me sleep.

Not only my mind, I had to admit. It was my soul as well. What had happened in Wycliffe had shaken me more than anything else I'd experienced in the short time I'd been with the Qaniss.

When the demons had attacked us on the other world, the experience had still had a surreal, dream-like quality to it. What had happened tonight, however, was very real. I could still recall every single moment with startling clarity. Everything from the way I'd felt when I'd realized demons were nearby to the anger and anxiety when I'd recognized Bram's presence.

The sight of him bloodied and chained. The rush of power when I'd opened the bond. What it had felt like to send Adonai's power into my weapons and kill the demons.

Realizing how close I'd come to losing Bram.

I settled a few feet away from him, leaning back against a tree. I didn't look directly at him, but I was aware of him, more aware than I'd ever been of another person. I wasn't just aware of him as a person though. It was so much more than that.

He'd told me to run. He'd known if I'd left, he'd be dead, and that it might kill me too, but he'd been willing to sacrifice his own life for the small chance I could survive. He'd wanted to protect me. But when he'd seen that I wasn't going to leave him, he'd fought with me. He hadn't tried to push me aside because I was too delicate. He'd accepted my strength. We'd worked together as one, and I couldn't begin to try to understand how that made me feel.

You were created to be bonded together, despite the impossibility of the hundreds of years separating you.

I rested my forehead on my knees. This was truly the reason I couldn't sleep. God had been patient with me, allowing me to bond with Bram and receive His power even though I wasn't sure what I believed. He'd given me the power to heal Bram when the other Qaniss had given him up for dead. And I knew the only reason Bram and I had survived tonight was because God, Adonai, whatever name He went by, had allowed it.

Why? I finally asked the question. *Why would you do any of that for me when I didn't accept You, didn't even want to acknowledge Your existence? When I've spent so much time being angry at You? Hating You?*

I knew the answer, of course. The same rote answer I'd heard sporadically through the last seventeen years. Love. But I hadn't been able to understand it then, and I still didn't think I could.

Why did Bram tell you to run? Why didn't you run? He'd said he'd been better off alone. You'd shut down the bond between the two of you. And, yet, you saved him at the risk of your own life. He'd been willing to die to give you a chance to live.

I knew the answer to that one too. *Because he loves me.*

He'd told me how he felt and why, but with our bond open, I didn't need him to say it at all. I could feel it, his love. And it wasn't some sort of mushy, head-in-the-air kind of thing. It was a fact. Solid. Reliable. He wanted to protect me, to be my partner in the truest sense of the word. It didn't matter how I felt about him because his love wasn't about feelings. It didn't change based on what I did. He could be furious with me, and he would still lay down his life for mine.

Who gave him the ability to love like that?

I wrapped my arms around my knees. *You*, I reluctantly acknowledged.

And if I could give a person the ability to have that kind of love, why wouldn't I have it myself?

I didn't say anything to that. There wasn't anything to say.

All you need to do is accept it. No hoops to jump through or things you have to do first. Accept it and strive to do as I ask you. It's not as complicated as most people think.

Was that really it? All I had to do was accept the truth? Accept that He loved me. That He'd died for me. And then try to do what He asked of me. Could it really be that easy? None of the churches I'd been forced to attend had ever made it sound like that. There'd always been rules to follow, and some of them had even contradicted each other.

Only read the King James Version of the Bible. No tattoos or piercings. Baptism as an adult only. Follow this dress code. Don't read / watch / listen to that. Talk this way. Don't do that. No speaking in tongues. You have to speak in tongues. Raise your hands. Close your eyes. Bow your head. Dance around. Stand still. Be quiet. Shout. Sit. Stand. Repeat after me...

It had always been about following the rules and making sure my behavior matched what others thought it should be.

It doesn't matter what others think you should do. Only what I tell you to do.

If I accepted that God was God, and I wasn't, then I accepted He was a Supreme Being with more knowledge and power than I could ever comprehend. I accepted He'd created everything, and had the power to destroy it all. If I accepted all of that, then I could accept He had authority over me, and that I needed to listen to what He said to do.

I could do it. I could believe and trust and obey. I knew it wouldn't be easy, but that's why it was a choice, not some warm-fuzzy thing. I could accept it, or I could walk away. I knew He wouldn't abandon me if I did the latter, but I wouldn't be in His will either.

Okay.

Relief like nothing I'd ever felt before went through me as soon as I said the word. It was as if everything I'd been carrying for the past seventeen years was suddenly lifted from my shoulders.

It was no longer about deciding between being good and being bad. It was only about obedience and disobedience. The choices were clear. It wasn't about picking out verses to say who was wrong and who was right, or whether or not something in the Old Testament was applicable today. It was only about obeying what He told me to do.

"Tempest?" Bram's voice came out of the darkness. The fire had died down at some point so I could only see the outline of his body. "What happened?"

His voice was low, but I knew if the others were close enough, they'd be able to hear him. I wasn't ashamed of my decision, but I wasn't ready to share it with all of them just yet. I did, however, need to tell Bram.

I moved the short distance between us so I was sitting next to him. He'd sat up and as I settled, I could see his face in the dim light.

"What you'd said before about me not being sure if God cares was true." I folded my hands on my lap and looked down at them. "And not only because of...what you saw." I took a moment to collect my thoughts. "I've never had a family, never had anyone to show me what unconditional love was. The God I was taught about growing up – whenever I happened to be with a home or family who said they believed – that God was all about behavior and trying to make me into the perfect little robot."

Bram shifted, but didn't say anything. I could feel him resisting the urge to use the bond to get a bit more deeply into what I was feeling, and I appreciated his restraint.

"I was never good enough for any of them. Not for the families I was placed with, not for the other kids in the homes. Never good enough for the churches I was taken to. For a long time, I assumed it was my fault. That I was a bad person, and everyone was right not to love me."

Bram's hand reached out and covered mine. His skin was warm and the touch reassuring. A surge of something so strong I couldn't deny it went through me. I kept it close, letting it give me the strength I needed to say the rest.

I raised a hand and brushed my finger across the scar on my right cheek. "When I was nine years-old, I was placed in a foster home where the family had a son who was fourteen. He hated me. He'd hit me, pinch me, try to...grab me. After a couple of weeks, I couldn't take it anymore. He tried to kiss me, and I slapped him. He grabbed a beer bottle off of the table, broke it and came after me. When he cut my face, I knew he was going to try to kill me, so I ran. By the time I was caught, he'd told his parents I'd attacked him, that the bottle had broken during the fight and I'd been cut. They believed him and I was sent back to the group home. With that kind of label, I knew no one would ever want me."

Bram's fingers tightened around my hand.

"I'd prayed to God the whole time I was there, prayed the parents would find out what their son was doing to me, and make him stop. I'd prayed someone would believe me."

"And it felt like Adonai didn't answer any of your prayers," Bram finished softly.

I shook my head. "I tried a couple times after that, to pray, to see if the God that everyone always talked about even cared. And then, when I was twelve, I was sent to live with..." My voice trailed off and I took a shaky breath. "What you saw in my nightmare, it really happened. More than once over the course of eighteen months. And I thought that meant God didn't care."

"What made you change your mind?" Bram asked.

"You," I said honestly. I met his eyes. "I can feel what you feel for me, and how nothing I could do could make you stop loving me."

His expression tightened, and I felt him start to pull back from the bond. It suddenly hit me that he was as scared of what he felt as I was. The knowledge gave me the strength to continue.

"If God created that bond, how could He not love at least that well? So I had to accept that if He loved me, there had to be a reason that all of that stuff happened to me, even if I can't understand it."

"What are you saying, Tempest?"

"I believe," I said it as simply as possible. "I know I'm not perfect and it's not going to be easy, but I believe."

I felt his relief, and only then realized how worried he'd been for me. Alongside that was something new. Not new from him, but new from me. I could feel that part of our bond that hadn't been solidified, the part only he had to bear. Now, however, I could feel something inside me reaching towards that part of him.

My stomach clenched. I'd been attracted to him from the first time I'd seen him. It had been impossible not to be. And even when I'd been angry at him, I'd had feelings for him. Crazy, mixed-up feelings, but feelings nonetheless. Then, I'd thought I'd lose him, and that had made me realize that, even without acknowledging it, I'd been falling for him. When I'd told the demons Bram was mine, I'd meant it in more ways than I'd wanted to admit.

Now I understood what it was. Along with my newfound faith, I wanted more.

I turned my hand in his so I could lace my fingers between

his. My heart was thudding loudly against my ribcage, and I knew Bram could feel all of the chaos of my emotions. I could hardly draw enough air to get the words out.

"I don't know if that changes anything for you, but I know it does for me."

Chapter Twenty-Six

Bram

She believed.

I knew she wasn't just saying it either. I could feel it, the change inside her. Something had shifted and she wasn't the same girl she'd been when we'd first met.

Then she threaded her fingers between mine, and what had been a comforting gesture turned into something else. Something I wasn't sure I wanted to consider. Being in love with her was painful enough.

"I don't know if that changes anything for you, but I know it does for me."

Her words pulled at the bond inside me, and I could feel it wanting to reach out, wanting to complete what I'd started. I hesitated, not wanting to read to much into her words. I'd waited so long for her, even before I'd known her, back when all I'd had was a prophecy about a person I'd been sure couldn't exist, I'd been waiting. And then I'd met her and she hadn't believed. Now, there was hope.

And I didn't want it.

I wanted her, yes, but I didn't want to hope she meant something more when she said it changed things for her.

Her face fell, and she pulled her hand away. "It's okay. I

understand."

Don't let her go.

I didn't even question it. I grabbed her wrist before she could move. "What do you understand?"

She didn't look at me. She looked at the place where my fingers were wrapped around her wrist. "I'd just thought–" She stopped and shook her head.

I could feel the churn of emotions as well as her trying to shield me from knowing what she was thinking.

"Talk to me, Tempest. Please." I'd never met someone so frustrating. At least Annabella said what she was thinking, even if I didn't like it.

"I thought because I believed, things would be different." She glanced up and then away. "It's okay though." She pulled her hand away and got to her feet.

I stared at her as she walked away.

Don't let her go.

I scrambled to my feet, wincing as my wounds twinged. *"Tempest, wait,"* I called out telepathically, not wanting to wake the others.

I felt her shock at the mental communication, and it was enough to let me catch up. I put my hand on her elbow ,and led her out of the clearing and a few steps into the woods. I understood it now.

"You think I don't..." I could barely make myself say it, it was so ridiculous. "Do you think I'm not in love with you anymore?"

"It's okay," she said again. She still couldn't look at me. "After what happened..."

"It's a love bond, Tempest. It doesn't go away."

"Do you want it to?"

There it was. I could feel it. Her real fear, one she hadn't wanted to voice. She thought it was an obligation, that I was here because I had to be.

"No." I let her feel the truth of what I was saying.

And it was true. Even when I'd been furious at her, when I'd been positive she'd never complete the bond, deep down, I hadn't wanted it gone. It was a part of me.

I had my own question to ask now. "Do you wish it was gone?"

She looked up at me, letting our eyes meet. "No, Bram. I don't wish it was gone."

Adonai, what do I do?

I knew what I wanted to do, but I also knew what I was afraid would happen if I did.

Trust me.

I was pretty sure those were my least favorite words when it came to Tempest.

Everything happens in My time.

I took a slow breath. My stomach was in knots, but I was going to do what He asked. I was going to trust Him.

I reached out slowly, giving her time to understand what I was doing and to step away if she wanted. I pushed back some of the curls that had fallen across her face. My fingers lightly touched her scar and I felt her body tense.

"When you said believing changed things for you," I spoke softly. "This is what you meant isn't it?"

She nodded. After a moment of silence, she frowned. "Are you going to make me say it?"

I smiled at the edge to her voice. There she was, the cocky girl who'd yelled at me for throwing an ax. I shook my head. "No, I'm not going to make you say it."

I leaned down and kissed her, a part of me still waiting for her to pull away. Instead, she put her arms around my neck and pulled me closer.

I'd kissed a couple girls back home in the few instances I'd tried to date, but there'd been no connection, nothing special.

This was completely different. I felt every bit of her, every cell in her body reacting to mine. Through the bond, I could feel what she was feeling. All of the pain from her past, her fear of the future...and something else that made my heart thud painfully against my chest.

I lifted my head, but put my arms around her waist, keeping her close. Her skin was flushed, the scar on her cheek standing out white against red.

"So." She blew out a breath. "That happened."

I laughed quietly and, for the first time since I'd found out about my world, about my mission, felt the tension ease from my body. It didn't matter what was coming. I wasn't alone anymore.

"Does this mean..." She hesitated, then finished her question. "Are we bonded? I mean, not like..."

"No. That's a choice you'll have to make." She opened her mouth, but I shook my head. "Not now. Take some time. You've had all of this pushed on you so fast."

"I can feel it," she said quietly. Her eyes got this faraway look and I knew she was reaching inside to where the bonds were rooted. "I can feel the...the love bond."

I couldn't stop the surge of emotion from going through me when she said it, but I didn't speak. I needed her to tell me what she was thinking.

"It's there, Bram. Inside me." She swallowed hard, the mask she always wore slipping. "But I'm scared."

I wondered if she'd ever said those words out loud before.

"I am too," I admitted.

"I hate being scared." She clenched her jaw.

I chuckled. "Me, too." I twisted a curl around my finger. "Angry's a lot easier, isn't it?"

She nodded and gave me a wry smile. "So what now?"

"Now, we go back, try to get some sleep, and then tomorrow we find demons to kill."

"I meant about...this." She shifted in my arms but didn't try to step away.

"We take it slow," I said. I let her go, but caught her hand before we moved too far apart. "I'm not going anywhere."

"But you're already bonded to me."

"And now I know you believe and you can feel the bond." I wanted to kiss her again, but resisted. She needed to know I hadn't only wanted her to believe because of how I felt. "I'll wait as long as you need me to, because once you choose, it's forever." I brushed my lips across the back of her knuckles. "And that's worth waiting for."

She squeezed my hand and walked with me back to the fire. It wasn't until I sat back down that I realized my wounds hurt less. I wasn't completely healed, but it seemed like what had happened between Tempest and I had sped things up.

I looked over at her where she sat next to me, and waited for her to make the next move. When she stretched out in front of me, I laid down behind her, sliding an arm around her waist. She didn't say anything, but her body relaxed against mine, and a few minutes later, she was asleep. It took me a bit longer, but finally, I joined her.

Chapter Twenty-Eight

Tempest

"It's started. Everyone up!"

I jerked awake almost immediately, and had about two seconds to remember that Bram's arm was around my waist before it was gone. He was up, wings out, expression serious. He held out a hand to me without looking down and I took it, letting him pull me to my feet, my own wings flicking nervously out behind me.

"What's happened?" Bram asked.

It had been Leigh, I saw now, who'd woken us. She and Lucan both looked worried.

"We were patrolling when we heard sirens. The police have been called to Wycliffe Christian School. They're saying some men have taken it hostage."

"It's not men, is it?" I asked, my stomach clenching.

Leigh shook her head and made a face. "We could smell them."

I remembered the scent from last night, and shuddered as the rest of the memories came back. My wings stretched out, the tips brushing against Bram's the same way I would've with my hand if I hadn't wanted to make sure my hands were free.

"What do we do?" I asked.

"Suit up," Annabella said, her voice grim. "I hope that arm's healed because it feels like we're going to need everyone." She gave me a once-over, but at least managed not to sneer. "No matter how badly they fight."

"She did plenty of damage last night," Bram snapped at her.

I flushed and turned away from Annabella to go through the weapons Bram and I had brought. I tucked a pair of knives into my boots, and my switchblade went into its usual spot at the small of my back. I straightened, and glanced over at Bram. He smiled at me as he slid his sword into the sheath on his back.

Instantly, warmth spread through me. It was weird, I thought. I knew we were going to battle, and now I knew the truth of what that meant, but one look from Bram made me feel stronger, like anything was possible. I glanced at the others, but they didn't seem to notice that anything had changed between Bram and I. Then Tady sent a smile my way, and I knew that she'd figured it out.

I gave her a small smile back as I stepped up to Bram's side. My heart began to race at the thought of what we were walking into, but before I could truly get worked up, a wave of calm went over me, and I knew it came from Bram. I shot him a grateful look as we waited for the others to finish getting ready.

You need more power.

Not exactly the encouragement I'd been hoping to hear from God right before a battle.

You are the Twelve, unlike any Qaniss who have ever lived. You are the direct descendant of an original founder. Together, you would be the most powerful group of Star Riders the worlds have ever known.

I glanced at Bram, wondering if he was hearing any of this.

No, Tempest. It's you who has to do this. You have to get them to stand together. To stand with you, and receive the power of the prophecy.

"All right," Bram said. "It's time to go." He looked at Leigh and Lucan. "You two lead the way. Slow when we get within a hundred yards. We'll spread out then, and get an idea of where everything is."

Tell them.

Great, my first group mission, and God wanted me to act like I knew everything.

Not everything. Just this.

An image flashed into my mind. Us, as a group, standing in a circle, our hands clasped I didn't get to see what the end result was. I only knew this was what God wanted.

"Um." I stopped and cleared my throat. Bram turned his

attention towards me and the others did the same. I was pretty sure they thought I was going to ask a question, or say I'd changed my mine. "God...I mean, Adonai, He wants us to do something." I almost scowled. I hated how uncertain I sounded.

"Excuse me?" Annabella stared at me.

"Adonai, He told me we need to...well, we need to do something before we go."

"We don't have time for this, Bram," Annabella said. She looked at Grady.

"She's right," Grady agreed. "If there are demons in the school, we have to get there as soon as possible."

"Let's hear her out," Bram said.

"Why?" Annabella asked. "She's not one of us, not really. She wasn't raised in our ways, listening to Adonai."

"She's a believer, Annabella," Bram said. "And a Qaniss. We listen to our own."

"I agreed to follow you, Bram, because that's how we always did things." Annabella took a step forward. Her dark eyes darted over to me, and then went back to Bram. "Maybe we need to change things."

"Annabella," Leigh said quietly.

"You really want to do this? Now?" Bram's shoulders stiffened. "We don't have the time. We need to get going."

"What we need," Annabella said. "Is a leader we can trust. One who isn't so distracted by a girl that he forgets his responsibility to Adonai. A leader we can follow into battle. And you're not it."

Chapter Twenty-Nine

Bram

"Back off!" Tempest snapped as she took a half-step in front of me. Her hands were clenched into fists, wings flaring.

Annabella took a step forward and I saw Grady tensing as well. A surge of protectiveness went through me, and I put my hand on Tempest's arm. The last thing we needed was a fight between the four of us, and that would be the least of what would happen. Because if Leigh tried to stop things, then Lucan would be in it too, and that was half of us fighting each other instead of going after the demons.

"Both of you, stop." The words came out louder than I'd intended, but it at least had the effect I wanted. Everyone looked at me.

Everyone including Tempest.

I could feel the surprise and the hurt coming across the bond, but I didn't take the time to reassure her. We didn't have the time.

Bram...

We didn't have the time.

"I've taken the oath." I kept my eyes on Annabella. "And you will fall in line. Is that understood?"

For several long seconds, she didn't say anything, only

stared at me with those black eyes of hers. Then, she nodded. "I'll follow," she agreed. "But if you screw this up, we're going to have this out."

I didn't even bother to dignify that with a response.

"Let's go." I looked at Leigh and Lucan, giving them a nod.

I could feel my bond twisting, and knew I needed to make things right. I turned towards Tempest, but she didn't look at me. Then Leigh and Lucan were setting off at a brisk run, and there was no time for anything else.

Bram...

No time for anything else.

The twelve of us ran through the woods, wings tucked tight as we dodged around the trees. It didn't take long before the stench of demons reached us, and we didn't need anyone to lead the way, but we stayed in formation, not spreading out until we were nearly at the school itself.

Tempest and I went around the front while the others moved to various vantage points to see what we were up against.

The police had already set up a barricade, and I knew without asking that they were now trying to figure out how to establish contact with the kidnappers so they could find out what the demands were. I wished I could walk over and tell them there wouldn't be demands, or that even if demands were made, things would still end with blood and chaos. But, of course, I couldn't. Even if they believed in the existence of demons, they'd never believe what was really happening in that school. And even if they did, there wasn't anything they could do about it.

We were the demon killers. The last of our kind.

Tempest and I stood at the edge of the forming crowd, listening for anything that could help us. I wasn't entirely sure what that could be, but I hoped I'd know it when I heard it. I'd fought a lot of demons in my life, but I'd never had to deal with something like this.

"Excuse me."

"Excuse me."

"Excuse me."

I did a double-take as three identical auburn-haired young woman shouldered their way past me. They went straight to a dark-haired woman who was standing at the edge of the police line.

"Aunt Noreen." The first girl threw her arms around the older woman. "Do they know anything yet?"

"No." The woman opened her arms to include the other two. "But your parents are talking to the chief." Her expression was fierce. "Your sisters are going to be fine."

My wings twitched against my back, and I had to force them to stay down. I wanted to fight. I wanted to tell those girls and their aunt that I'd save their family. That no one was going to die today.

Before I could say any of those things, I felt a sudden stab of fear and it didn't come from me. I spun around and saw that Tempest's face had gone white. I followed her gaze and my stomach lurched. A *beach cliseadh* was hovering over one of the windows, but it was what was in the window that made me want to throw up.

A *vihane surma* stood in front of the window. In front of it was a terrified little girl, her wide, dark eyes filled with tears.

My heart pounded, the sound of blood rushing in my ears.

It wasn't smart. It wasn't even only a little bit dumb. This was massively stupid, but I was still going to do it.

I drew my sword, and unfurled my wings. The sounds of surprise from the crowd were only background noise. I was aware of Tempest reacting, her actions almost like an extension of my own. My attention, however, wasn't on her. It was focused on the demons I could see, the ones I could feel.

I flapped my wings, letting them carry me up above the crowd. I raised my sword.

"*Havoc!*" I shouted the word as loud as I could, knowing the others would hear me.

We weren't going in there, nice and quiet, risking the lives of all of the children and the staff. There was no Council anymore to say we had to tiptoe about. It was my decision now, and I was going to make the demons come after me, take this fight somewhere we wouldn't risk collateral damage.

"*Bram!*" Tempest shouted into my mind. I glanced down and saw her trying to fight her way through the chaos that had erupted below.

Like I'd said, not my smartest move.

But it was too late to take it back now.

"*Fly!*" I caught a glimpse of darkness starting to stream from the school as the demons took on their more ethereal, invisible form. The humans didn't see them, but their screams said they felt the evil.

I sheathed my sword as I turned, and hoped Tempest would listen. A moment later, I saw her launch herself into the air. Out of the corner of my eye, I caught glimpses of the others, all flying now. I was going to hear it from Annabella when this was all over, but first we had to take care of our business. I'd deal with the fallout later.

I could hear the demons behind me and knew I had to think fast. I hadn't been thinking at all when I'd pulled my little stunt, and now the twelve of us were being chased by an unknown number of demons. I looked down, searching for somewhere to set down, to make a stand.

We were at least a couple miles away from the school when I finally saw something we could use. I let myself drop towards it, and knew the others would follow. The clearing was big enough for us to fight, and an old barn at the far end could watch our back.

I landed first and pulled my sword out again. The others landed behind me, spreading out in a semi-circle. Tempest was at my left, knives in her hands. I wished I'd had more time to train her, but there wasn't anything I could do about that now. I'd just have to protect her as best I could.

The *ardens lingua* landed first, taking on their corporeal form. The others followed quickly. *Excoriator*, *spinis*, *cropian llyngyr*, *beach cliseadh*, and *vihane surma*. All six species of demons I knew of were crowded together. As each new one materialized, my heart sank a little lower. How many of these things were here?

I pushed Adonai's power into my sword, and waited for the demons to make the first move. Reacting wasn't my usual way of fighting, but we were more outnumbered than I'd realized, and I knew we needed to conserve our energy.

It was one of the *beach cliseadh* who moved first, as if hovering over the group was too much for it. It swooped down towards Kassia, and she knocked it aside with her wing.

As if that was some sort of signal, the demons rushed us all at once, and I lost sight of the rest of my people. The blur of battle came over me, and I let everything else fall away. My body moved without me really having to think about it.

Wings hit against demon flesh, pushed away *spinis* and *excoriator*. My sword cut through *vihane surma* wrists and necks, took off *spinis* arms and legs. I spun and dodged, trying to avoid *ardens lingua* blood and *vihane surma* touch.

I was aware of Tempest beside me, viciously lashing out with her knives, using her wings in ways I'd never seen. She was an amazing fighter, better than she'd been when I'd been training her. I didn't know if it was because she'd finally accepted who she was, or if her belief in Adonai had opened her up, but whatever it was, she was doing more than holding her own.

Except it wasn't enough.

Pain sliced bright and hot across my arm, but it wasn't my pain. It was hers. I let out an angry half-growl, and took out the *excoriator* who'd cut her.

As I turned to make sure she was okay, the rest of the fight cut through the haze.

We were losing.

Bram!

Adonai's voice slammed into me.

I didn't need Him to tell me I'd screwed up. I knew it. And if I couldn't figure out a way to save everyone, the mission Adonai had given us would be over just as we'd accomplished the first part.

It's not you who'll do the saving. I chose her for a reason.

He was right. Of course.

"Fall back!" I shouted as loud as I could. "Fall back!"

I grabbed Tempest's arm and pulled her after me. I only hoped Annabella would be able to get some defenses up so I could tell them all what we needed to do.

Or at least tell them I had no idea what I was doing.

Chapter Thirty

Tempest

I hurt. A lot.

The minute I'd seen Bram launch himself into the air, I'd known we were in trouble. But, he was my bonded and that meant I was going to follow him, even into trouble. I'd sent a quick prayer up to Adonai to help us, and then I'd taken off.

We'd landed in a clearing, and I'd felt Bram's shock as the demons landed. Then we'd started to fight, and I'd known this was it. I used my knives and my wings, pushing power through both to take out as many demons as I could, but when one fell, another was there to take its place.

I'd never really thought about how many demons existed in the world until now. I'd been in church enough to know there were twice as many angels as there were demons, but that kind of thing didn't really acknowledge the vast number of demons that existed.

I hissed out a breath as an *excoriator* claw sliced through the sleeve of my shirt and into the flesh underneath. It wasn't deep enough to keep me from cutting the demon's arm off, but it still hurt.

"Fall back!"

Bram was yelling from somewhere to my right.

"Fall back!"

I obeyed, backing my way towards the bar. Out of the corner of my eye, I saw a bloodied Annabella doing something I sincerely hoped was putting up protection, because if we didn't have it, the old barn wasn't going to do much to keep the demons from getting to us. I felt something shiver around me as I reached the barn and Tady opened the door. We hurried inside and Bair closed the doors behind us. He put down a thick beam across the double doors, but we all knew that wasn't what would keep the demons out.

The ceiling had enough holes that I had light enough to see the others when I looked around. A wave of relief went through me as I counted eleven. We were all here. Bloody, bruised, wounded and exhausted, but alive and here.

"Those aren't going to hold for long."

I looked over at Annabella. She had a streak of blood across her cheek and, judging by the way she was holding her ribs, probably a couple of cracked or broken bones. The rest looked just as bad. My own shoulder was throbbing in time with my pulse, and I knew it was only a matter of time before I dislocated it again. I'd healed faster than I should have been able to, but it was still tender. Then again, if we all died here, my shoulder wouldn't exactly be a problem anymore.

"I'm sorry," Bram said. "This is all my fault."

No one agreed with him, but no one argued either, letting their silence speak for them.

Tempest.

"It's all our faults," I spoke up. Everyone looked at me as I continued, "Bram may be the leader, but we all chose to follow. We should've spoken up." I met Bram's eyes. "*I* should have said something."

"You did," he began.

I shook my head. "I could've done more. I could have refused to come until you listened to what God wanted us to do."

"She's right."

I turned. If Leigh hadn't been standing in my line of sight, I would've thought the comment had come from her, but she hadn't said a word. In fact, she was staring at her twin along with the rest of us.

Annabella's dark eyes were fierce, her cheeks flushed. "We're the Qaniss. Chosen by Adonai from birth. We've experienced His power all our lives. We've seen what He can do and how He uses us." She looked directly at me. "We know the prophecy of the Twelve. We were wrong to discount what you said." She took a breath. "*I* was wrong."

"What do we need to do?" Bram asked, his voice quiet.

I swallowed hard. I couldn't do this. Who was I to tell these experienced warriors what to do? They'd been fighting demons for years, had been training for it their whole lives. I was some kid from Ohio who'd only started believing in all of this a few days ago.

I chose you. You are the Twelfth. This is what I created you to do. To be.

I supposed I should've found it comforting, but I didn't. In fact, it scared the crap out of me.

I didn't say it to bring you comfort. I said it to remind you. Serving Me is never comfortable.

"Tempest." Bram was standing right in front of me. He pushed back some hair that had fallen out of my hasty ponytail. "I'm sorry. I should have listened to you. Adonai made you my bonded, and I should have trusted you."

I nodded, not trusting myself to speak to him. There were so many things I wanted to say, some angry, some sweet enough to make me blush.

"Tell us what Adonai wants us to do," he said, dropping his hand.

I could feel his confidence in me, his certainty that I could do this, and it gave me strength. "Stand in a circle."

As we moved, something hit the barn with enough force to make it shudder. I glanced at Annabella and saw her expression tighten. Her protection wasn't going to last much longer. I could only pray it would be long enough.

I took Bram's hand on my right and Fynn's on my left. The others copied me.

"Place your fingers on the tattoos."

On Bram's side, a jolt went through me, and his fingers tightened on mine, telling me he'd felt it too.

You can do this. Bram's voice echoed in my head.

I took a slow breath and closed my eyes. I didn't speak out loud, and my prayer was simple. I could only hope it'd be enough.

Adonai, help Your chosen.

For a moment, everything stopped.

The noise from the demons was gone. No wind. The clouds stopped moving. It was like the world around us had frozen in time. Even my own heartbeat, my own breath, hung in suspension. Then the earth tilted, the air pulled together in a rush.

And exploded out in a rush of white heat.

It was similar to what I'd experienced when Bram and I had bonded, but so much more. This was the presence of the same God who had told Moses he could only see His back. The power that had resided in the Holy of Holies, that lived in the Ark of the Covenant.

It filled me, went through me, covered me. It made me

nothing and everything.

I could feel the power of creation, and I understood what it had taken to make the universe, all of the universes. I felt the enormity of the love He had for His creation, and what He had done for mankind.

And I knew this was still only a fraction of what Adonai had, that if He had given any more, our finite minds and mortal bodies would never be able to contain it.

Then, it receded, and I opened my eyes. The excess power had burned away, but I knew each of us had retained enough to make us more powerful than any Qaniss had ever been. I didn't know what this meant for us in the future, but for now, it meant we could fight. My wounds were healed and my fatigue gone.

I looked over at Bram and saw the same knowledge in his eyes. We broke the circle, but Bram and I kept our fingers linked, waiting.

Something was wrong.

I frowned, and then saw Bram do the same. I knew he was sensing that something had changed. I wasn't sure what until Leigh spoke.

"I don't hear them anymore."

She was right, I realized with a start of surprise. That sense of time pausing had gone, but the noise from outside hadn't come back yet. Annabella glanced at Bram, and he nodded. We each drew our weapons, and I saw I hadn't been the only one healed. We were all still covered with blood and dirt, but none of us appeared to be injured.

Grady moved forward first, and lifted the bar across the doors. He set it aside quietly, and then fell back to Annabella's side. Tady and Bair stepped up to the doors, and each took a handle. They looked at Bram and he nodded. As the pair pulled the doors open, the rest of us braced ourselves.

And nothing happened.

Cautiously, Bram and I stepped outside.

Nothing.

No, not nothing, I realized as I looked down. The grass was covered in ash. Heaps of ash over the entire clearing.

"*Deo gratias,*" Tady breathed out the words behind me.

The demons were gone, disintegrated into ash. I looked around at the others for an explanation, but they looked as stunned as I felt.

"Bram." My voice was shaking slightly. "What happened?"

"I don't know." He shook his head. "I've never heard of anything like this."

I turned towards him, my stomach twisting. I wasn't afraid of Adonai using this power to hurt us, but I also remembered what He'd told me, that serving Him wasn't comfortable. I knew what He hadn't said as well. That serving Him could be dangerous.

Bram sheathed his sword, and reached out to me. I let him draw me into his arms, let him give me his strength and his confidence. His faith in me and in Adonai. He wrapped his wings around us, giving us a bit of privacy from the others.

"Are you okay?" he asked as he cupped the side of my face.

I leaned into his touch. "I'm not sure," I admitted. "What did I do?"

"I don't know," he said again. "But we'll figure it out. We're in this together. You're not alone anymore." He smiled. "I'm not alone anymore."

My heart did a funny skipping beat as he bent his head to kiss me. My arms tightened around his waist as my eyes closed. I could feel the love bond between us slowly twining together, but I knew it wouldn't be fully complete until we did the ceremony. There wasn't any time for that right now though. I would let myself enjoy these few moments of comfort, but we'd have to rejoin the others soon. We needed to figure out exactly what had happened, how Adonai's power had changed us, and what we were going to do next.

I wasn't anxious though. I knew there would be times in

the future where that wouldn't be the case, but for right now, in this moment, I knew I was safe. As for what came next, I knew Bram had my back, and that the others would be at my side as well. I wasn't simply one person anymore, me against the world. I was one of twelve, one of The Twelve, and I knew our story was only beginning.

Made in the USA
Middletown, DE
04 August 2017